THE MEDDLERS

by Teddi Robinson

To Judy

Merry Christmas

Teddi Robinson
Dec 17, 2012

a BlackWyrm book
Louisville, Kentucky

THE MEDDLERS

A BlackWyrm Book
BlackWyrm Publishing
10307 Chimney Ridge Ct, Louisville, KY 40299

Printed in the United States of America.

ISBN: 978-1-61318-100-3
LCCN: 2011903305

Second edition: March 2011

CHAPTER 1

Life has a way of changing your plans, thought Melanie as she waited for James. *It is so pleasant here in the meadow sitting on the blanket under the poplar tree.* Melanie tried to read her book and look relaxed, but she twisted her hair and every so often she would finger the ring she wore around her neck. This was the ring James had given her on her 16th birthday, as he asked her to be his girl.

Where is James? She wondered. He is never late and it is ten minutes past the time he was to be here. Could he have had an accident? Did his mother have another bad spell? Did his father find out that he is meeting me and make him stay home? Where is he?

***

James kept dilly-dallying because of the news that he had to tell Melanie. He knew the news would hurt her but he hoped she would forgive him.

James started to remember the first time he saw Melanie. It was a day much like today; sun shining, light breeze, and the birds singing at the top of their lungs. The meadow was beautiful with the green grass and the poplar trees in bloom. He saw her run through the meadow and he hid behind a poplar tree. Then he heard her fall. Yep, it was the same rock; he'd fall over, if he wasn't careful.

When James realized Melanie wasn't hurt, James asked, "Are you all right?"

Melanie was extremely sky and didn't answer.

"What's the matter? Did the cat steal your tongue and won't give it back? Sorry if I laughed, but I used to fall over that rock a lot."

Melanie realized this boy, from out of nowhere, was only being friendly. "No, but my knee hurts."

"Okay, I'll see that you get home. You just might fall again. Where do you live?"

"I don't live very far from here. My dad works for Mr. Smith. Do you know him? We moved here a few days ago. I'm Melanie Cox. What is your name?"

"I'm James Smith and Mr. Smith is my dad. I guess we'll be seeing a lot of each other." As they walked James was thinking. *She sure is pretty. Her black, curly hair looks like fine silk and the way the sun catches the shine, makes it look like dots of small diamonds. She has a cute little nose that turns up at the end and those blue eyes! I think this is to be a beautiful friendship.*

Melanie was thinking, *I like him, and I know we are going to be good friends. We already have something in common, the rock I fell over. He is handsome with his brown hair. I like the way the front lock keeps falling over his eye. His brown eyes look gentle. They certainly showed concern over my knee. I know he has been in the sun a lot by his tan.*

***

James' father, Tom Smith, realized too late that James was getting serious about Melanie. He decided to have a talk with James, the first chance he got. Just then, James sees his father and walks over to him.

Before James can say anything, Mr. Smith says, "James, I realize how much you enjoy Melanie's company and that you think she is everything you want in a wife. However, you must realize that her folks are share croppers, and they move from farm to farm and from plantation to plantation. Their work here is finished, and they will be moving shortly. Your great-grandfather settled this farm and our family has been here ever since. Do you think oil and water will mix or in this case a gypsy and a farmer? Please think about it."

"Dad, I have thought about it, and I know that Melanie loves this place as much as I do. Therefore, I know that we have a future here on the farm."

This wasn't the answer Mr. Smith, was looking for and he exploded! "I forbid you to see or talk to Melanie Cox again. If I hear of you talking to or seeing her, I'll thrash you within an inch of your hide. Then I'll blackball the Coxes from getting another job on any farm or plantation for miles around. Do you understand me? There is no future for you and Melanie, not here, not anywhere."

James said nothing, but he was thinking, *I'll ask Melanie to marry me. I've spent so much time with dad that I am going to be late meeting Melanie.*

CHAPTER 2

James saw Melanie under the tree and thought, *my but she is pretty! I'm so lucky that she agreed to be my girl. Now I must leave her.* "Hi, hon, sorry I'm late, but I got busy and forgot to watch the time. Have you been waiting long?"

"No, I haven't, but I was beginning to worry that maybe you had an accident."

"Honestly, I was dreading to see you because I have some news that will hurt you, but I'm hoping that you will forgive me." With the pain showing on his face, he lowered his head and said, "I joined the Army and will be leaving in a few days. I really would like for you to write to me. Will you marry me when I get out of the Army?"

"Oh, James, I would wait for you forever. I'll write to you every day and yes, I'll marry you. I love you so very much."

"And I love you. Rubbing his hand over his eyes, James asks, "Shall we go tell our parents?"

Melanie lowered her eyes and said, "Before we tell your parents, I have been dreading to tell you something. My father has accepted a job close to Lexington, Kentucky. It is a horse farm called Dream On. We'll be moving shortly."

At this moment Mr. Smith appeared, and said, "I see the Coxes aren't moving a moment too soon."

James replied, "Dad, I've joined the Army and will be leaving in a few days. After I've saved some money, Melanie and I will be married. I hope to have your blessing. After I've served my time in service, I would like to come back to the farm with my wife."

Turning red in the face, Mr. Smith exploded, "As far as I'm concerned, you can leave now. I HAVE NO SON!"

With all the calm James could muster he replied, "Okay, Dad, but I want to tell mom, and I want Melanie with me when I do."

Mr. Smith yelled, "Neither one of you is welcome in my house and may your lives be cursed from this moment on."

CHAPTER 3

On arriving at the house James says, "Please wait here on the porch, and we will come for you in a few minutes."

"Okay, love, but try to hurry. Your father may come home at any minute. I just don't want to be where he can yell at me."

"I'll hurry, and everything will be Okay. You'll see."

James and his mother came out of the house. Mrs. Smith walked over to Melanie, held out her arms, and said, "I've watched you grow from a lovely child to a beautiful and graceful woman. I'm so happy to have a daughter-in-law whom my son loves deeply. Welcome, Melanie, and if you need anything just let me know."

Melanie was overwhelmed with love and gratitude.

"Thank you, Mrs. Smith. I will strive to be the kind of wife James deserves and to be the kind of daughter-in-law to make you proud."

Mrs. Smith thought a few minutes and said, "Melanie, since you are going to be part of the family and I could use some help, would you consider living here with us?"

Again Melanie was speechless but managed to say, "What would Mr. Smith say?"

Mrs. Smith put a reassuring arm around Melanie and said, "Don't you worry about that. I'll take care of Tom. He won't give you any trouble. Now the two of you had better go tell Mr. and Mrs. Cox your plans."

***

What a revolting turn of events, thought Tom Smith as he walked toward the woods! The woods always helped Tom to calm down and to think out problems rationally.

Tom was thinking, *I have always hoped that James would marry Susan Brown. Her father, Sam, has the largest farm in the county and with my farm, we would have the largest farm in the state. Nope, James' marriage to this... this nobody will not do.*

Out loud Tom prayed, "God, please help me. Help me show my son that his marriage to Melanie will not work. Thank you God, for having the Coxes move to Kentucky in a few days. Amen."

Here's what I'll do, thought Tom, *I'll have Jane invite the Coxes to dinner. Then James will see that Melanie could never fit into our social life. A share cropper's daughter... NEVER, NEVER, NEVER!*

CHAPTER 4

Melanie and James found Mr. Cox in the hay barn. Melanie said, "Dad, James and I need to talk to you and mom. Could you spare a few minutes to come up to the house?"

Buddy Cox said, "Go on up to the house, and I will be up in a few minutes."

When Melanie and James entered the kitchen door, Mrs. Cox looked at them and said, "I have been expecting you. Have you spoke to your dad?"

"Yes, mother," Melanie answered, "Dad will be here in a few minutes."

Melanie and James exchanged glances as Mr. Cox entered the room.

Buddy Cox said, "Okay, spit it out. I need to go back to work"

James looks at Melanie, clears his throat and says, "Mr. and Mrs. Cox, Melanie has been my constant companion for the last six years. We have grown from friendship to a loving relationship. I will be leaving in a few days for basic training in the Army. I have asked Melanie to wait for me, and when I have saved some money, we will be married. We would like your blessing." Before anyone could say anything, James continued, "As you know my mother is not well and she would like for Melanie to be her companion until our wedding day."

Jane Cox was overwhelmed. Jane had anticipated the wedding announcement for a long time. *Never in my wildest dreams did I dream Mrs. Smith would open her heart and home to Melanie.* She said, "You have my blessing. I have expected this for some time."

Buddy finally spoke, "I would be delighted to have James as a son-in-law. However, I must tell you that marriage is a long hard road. You have to love each other in both the good and the bad times. There will be people who will try to destroy your love for each other. Also, if you do marry, these same people will try to destroy your marriage.

"As for Melanie to become Mrs. Smith's companion, I don't think so. The job in Kentucky is for a farm hand and two cooks. This is a large horse farm with 40 farm hands. Melanie will be cooking for the men who take care of the horses and my wife will be cooking for the main house."

Jane put her two-cents in, "Love conquers all, and I'm sure God will give you both the strength and wisdom to overcome any obstacles. Welcome to our family, James. The decision on whether Melanie will stay with Mrs. Smith or go with us, is your first major decision."

Buddy, with his mouth wide open, was thinking, *How could Jane say the decision was up to these two, not dry behind the ears, kids?*

Buddy just shook his head and said, "I've got to go back to work." And out the door he went.

Mrs. Cox looks from Melanie to James and says, "James, would you and Melanie like to have a cup of coffee? We could discuss the pros and cons of your wedding plans. Maybe you haven't started thinking of the kind of wedding you want."

"Mom, I think that is a great idea. Don't you, James?"

"Sure, and coffee sounds great." James replies.

***

On the way back to the barn, Buddy was thinking, *Mr. Smith isn't going to make it easy for these two kids, I'm sure. Why, he may even disown James. Then what would they do? I guess they'd survive. Jane and I started our married life on my daddy's farm. We lost everything, when the dust storms hit Kansas in 1935. We had never seen anything like that before or since. The dust swirled around and covered everything. It was so thick; sometimes you couldn't see your hand in front of your face. When the wind and the dust finally settled down, the top soil on the farm had blown away. It was a terrible sight; no crops, no grass, and the trees were covered with dust and debris. Melanie was 12 years old and quite a beauty. Thank God, I got the job with Tom Smith. Most of our friends didn't get work and had to live in tents. Jane has been great through this whole experience. Melanie is the exact replica of Jane, right down to the turned-up nose. I can't believe that we have been married for 20 years. Jane and I went to school together, and I think I loved her the first time I laid eyes on her. Yes, God has been good to us. I pray that God will be as good to James and Melanie.*

CHAPTER 5

As Kitty Smith was preparing supper, she was reviewing the arguments in favor of the marriage. The toughest one would be for Melanie to move in and become a companion to her. Kitty was thinking, I know how Tom feels about share croppers, and I know that he won't want Melanie for a daughter-in-law. Tom and I met when he came to work for my father as a share cropper. He'll just have to remember how my father reacted to our marriage. Dad was as much against our marriage as Tom is against James'. It took several years, but tom finally won my father over. When dad died, they were best friends.

***

After WWI, Tom Smith went to visit some friends in Tennessee. Tom thought the Tennessee hills and valleys were beautiful. When the train went through Jackson, Tom knew this was where he wanted to settle.

Several men were standing outside the general store and Tom walked over to them. Tom said, "I really like the area, and I would like to stay, but I need a job. Would you know of one? I was raised on a farm, and I would be an asset to anyone who hired me."

One gentleman stepped forward, looked Tom up and down, and said, "Sure, I'd like to hire you, but I can't offer much in the way of money. I can offer you three meals a day and a place to stay. At the end of the harvest, we'll split the profits 60/40, 60 percent for me and 40 percent for you."

Extending his hand, Tom says, "My name is Tom Smith, and I'll make your farm very profitable for both you and me. Just tell me your name, how to get to your place, and when do I start?"

Shaking hands with Tom, the gentleman says, "I'm Jud Spencer. My place is about two miles south of here. I'll show you the way in a few minutes, and you can start now. The supplies should be ready to load in the wagon. So go inside and tell Mr. Grant that you are working for me. He'll tell you what to do and I'll be along shortly."

CHAPTER 6

Kitty Spencer saw her dad and a strange man coming up the road. Kitty wondered, *who has dad got with him? Maybe dad finally found a hired hand. I guess I'll know soon enough.*

After unloading the wagon, Mr. Spencer brought Tom to the house.

"Tom, I want you to meet my daughter, Kitty. Kitty, this is Tom Smith. He will be staying here and helping me work the farm. Hope you don't mind."

Kitty stammered, "No, dad, I don't mind at all," and she was thinking, *my, oh my, he is good looking! I always joked about waiting for a tall, dark, handsome man, but never thought I meet one. I like his black curly hair and his eyes are a pale blue. The tan just makes his features more striking. I'm sure glad dad hired him.*

Kitty is so cute. Tom was thinking, *I'm going to try to get her to like me. She is so beautiful with her blond hair and grey eyes.* Tom said, "I'm glad to meet you." and he extended his hand.

Jud was watching with fearful eyes and thinking, *If I didn't need help so bad, I'd send this guy on his way. I can see right now that both my Kitty and this fellow are attracted to each other.*

***

A year later, the farm had returned to the way it was before the war and it prospered. Tom and Kitty had become friends, discovered they loved each other. The wedding was planned; friends, neighbors and relatives were invited to the biggest wedding reception to be held at the farm. Jud Spencer stood looking at his beautiful daughter and thought, *Tom isn't good enough for my Kitty. I've waited too long and now they are getting married. Guess the only thing I can do is grin and bear it.*

***

It took awhile but Tom and Mr. Spencer became the best of friends. Mr. Spencer was heard telling anyone, who would listen, "I couldn't have made the farm what it is today without Tom's help. He is a very good husband to my Kitty and one of my best friends."

CHAPTER 7

Mrs. Cox walking from the mailbox had a very surprised look on her face. She had an invitation in her hand and was turning it over and over. She was thinking, *Buddy will be so surprised to see the invitation from the Smith's. I can't believe they are giving Melanie and James an engagement party. Maybe, Buddy is wrong about Mr. Smith.*

Seeing Buddy in the field, Mrs. Cox, rushes to him and says, "An engagement party for the kids, Isn't that wonderful? Of course we'll go."

Buddy takes her in his arms and says, "Maybe, I misjudged Mr. Smith. It'll give you a chance to wear your pettiest dress, go to a party, and get to know the Smith's a little better."

Kissing her husband, Mrs. Cox turns toward the house and says, "I've got a million things to do, so I'll see you later. Love ya."

***

Sitting at the kitchen table, Mrs. Cox is making a list of things to do for the party.

1. Wash and Iron Buddy's best overalls.
2. See if I can still get into my good party dress. If not then, I'll have to alter it.
3. Check to see if I have enough of the pretty flour sacks to make Melanie a dress.
4. Look at our finances. If enough, buy lace for her dress.
5. Design and make her dress.
6. Fix both Melanie's and my hair.

When the fifth thing on the list was finished, Mrs. Cox called Melanie to try on the dress.

Melanie took one look at the dress, hugged her mother, and exclaimed, "I love it. Mom, I will feel so out of place. What will I talk about? How can I make James proud of me, when I don't know how to act around the owners, their wives, or their daughters?"

"Honey" Mrs. Cox says as she takes her in her arms. "Always remember, James loves you. Mrs. Smith wants you as a companion. She wants to do two things for you. First to get to know you better and second to teach you the social graces of the gentle folk. You will win Mr. Smith and others over by just being yourself. Just remember to always be a lady, trust in God, and never doubt James' love for you."

CHAPTER 8

James arrived to escort Melanie and her parents to the party. James took one look at Melanie and said, "Melanie, you look so beautiful. You'll be the envy of every girl and all the guys will wonder what you see in me."

Melanie blushed and murmured, "Thank you."

***

As soon as they arrived at the party, Mrs. Smith came to greet them.

Mrs. Smith put her arms around Melanie and said, "You look so pretty and I really like the design of your dress."

To which Melanie answered, "Thank you. My mother designed and made the dress for me. I'd like you to meet my mother, Jane Cox, and my father, Buddy Cox. This is Kitty Smith, James' mother."

Turning to Mrs. Cox, She asked, "Do you think you could design and make the dresses for the wedding? I would furnish the material, a place for you to work, and pay you for your time and labor."

Jane replied, "I would be honored to design and make the dresses, but really you don't have to pay me as this is my daughter's wedding."

The other guests started arriving, so Melanie and James stood between the two sets of parents, in the receiving line. Kitty and Tom introduced each guest to Melanie and her parents.

The women all wore beautiful gowns of silk and lace. Melanie felt all warm inside, because of the compliments Kitty Smith gave her and her mother.

***

The pig was roasting over the open pit. The tables were laden with all kinds of cooked and uncooked vegetables and salads. All kinds of deserts were on display, and there was plenty of lemonade, coffee, tea, soft drinks, and even some home-brew and wine. The fiddlers were on hand to play for the dancing and everyone was in a festive mood.

***

Everyone gathered in groups, ate, and talked. Then the fiddlers started to play. Before James had a chance to go to Melanie, Susan Brown was by his side. She looked up at James and batted her grey eyes at him and said, "James, you always have the first and the last dance with me. Should it be different tonight? You're not married yet... Are you? I know Melanie won't mind and she may not know how to dance. Does she?"

James thought, *how could I have ever thought about being serious with this ungracious, unladylike creature, who pretends to be my friend?* He didn't say what he was thinking but said instead, "Susan, you look stunning and I have always enjoyed dancing with you. Melanie is my love, my life, and my future. Therefore, not only is the first and last dance hers, but every dance in between. As far as Melanie not knowing how to dance, the subject never came up. But let me assure you, that it will be my pleasure to teach her to dance. By the way, isn't Melanie's dress beautiful on my girl?"

With a toss of her head, and sending daggers at Melanie, She tells him, "I guess I'd better line up some dances." As she walked away, she was thinking, *sorry, James, but I won't give you up without a fight.*

The conversation between James and Susan proved to Melanie and her parents, how much James loved and would go to protect her.

CHAPTER 9

James went to the Ft. Knox Military Base, Kentucky for his basic training. He was elated and thought *what a lucky break. The base is within driving distance to Lexington, Kentucky. I'll be able to see Melanie every time I have leave.*

***

Mr. Smith didn't accept the news of James' assignment and thought, *if Melanie had stayed with us, instead of going with her parents, I could have broken them up. Oh well, I'll just plan a trip to see James and maybe we will take several trips to Kentucky. I'll always take Susan with us. Then James can see the difference between Susan and Melanie. Melanie will never be our kind and he can't help but see it.*

CHAPTER 10

The farm in Lexington, Kentucky, was much larger than the Smith's farm in Tennessee. There were several white barns trimmed in red, with white cottages close by. The cottages are for the married employees and their families. The large bunk house is for the 40 men, horse trainers, horse groomers, and the jockeys. These men eat in a large kitchen called the mess hall. The main house is a brick federal style home with a long driveway lined with trees. The driveway circled in front of the house.

Mr. Cox's duties are to oversee the section of the farm that raises the hay, corn, vegetables, and the orchard. He oversees the maintenance of all the barns and the houses. Mrs. Cox's duties are to cook and oversee the staff in the main house. Melanie's assignment is to cook and clean for the men in the bunk house.

***

Melanie looked around the kitchen and thought, *My, it's big. I wonder if I'm up to doing a good job. Dad thought so, or he wouldn't have included me on the contract. Anyway, when I have time, I'll go out and watch the horses work out. I think the older men are trainers while the younger men are grooms and jockeys. The younger men look to be about my age. They'll be showing up at any time. Sure hope they like my cooking.*

***

The first man in the kitchen was John. He took one look at Melanie and said, "Hi, little lady, I'm John."

Melanie replied, "I'm Melanie, and I hope you like breakfast."

John just laughed and said, "You could serve burnt biscuits and raw eggs, and this group would tell you that you were the best cook in the world. These men aren't going to let you quit."

Melanie blushed and turned back to the stove. In Melanie's heart she thanked God for sending John in first. He had sent the butterflies flying from her stomach. Melanie was thinking, *John sure is a big man with no hair. I bet he is the same age as dad.*

John rises to leave and says, "I'll see you in a little while as I want to report to the men how good the breakfast is and how pretty you are."

***

As John entered the bunk house, he said, "You are in for a very pleasant surprise. Not only can this little girl cook, but she is a lady through and through, not bad looking either. Remember all the rules Hatchet Face, the former cook, put down? Well, this little lady deserves those rules. After you see and speak to her, you'll agree. Believe me, the food was good."

One of the guys speaks up, "You bet we remember Hatchet Face's rules! No smoking or chewing tobacco in the mess hall. Wipe your feet off before entering. Remove your hats. Wash your hands before eating. Also, breakfast is 4:30 a.m. Anyone entering after 4:45 a.m. will not be fed."

"Remember how she emphasized that rule by repeating..." Rowdy in a mock tone says, "and I REPEAT, they will not be fed, if anyone enters the mess hall after 4:45 a.m. Is this understood by everyone?"

It was John's turn to speak, "When you guys got to yourselves, you decided to break the rules, not all at once, but by taking turns and throwing such a fit that Hatchet Face would relent and let you eat."

"It worked! Didn't it? She finally quit. Thank God."

The men went to breakfast. Very little conversation, only eating, took up their time. Rowdy, being very shy, kept looking at Melanie, when he thought she wouldn't notice. He wondered, *Does she have a boyfriend?*

Back at the bunk house, Rowdy asked John, "You are right about the food. Do you know if she is spoken for?"

"No, I don't." John answered, "Why don't you ask her?"

"Okay, I will in due time, after I get to know her a little better."

CHAPTER 11

Relaxing in a chair, Tom Smith was looking out the window. He hadn't heard from James for a few days and missed him a lot. Tom reflected on the letter. *I was so frightened when I went to camp for the first time, during WWI. There was another soldier, with the same background as mine and we became instant friends. His name was Stanley Dunn. James told me his Captain's name is Stanley Dunn. I wonder if it is the same man I served with. I know Stanley stayed in the army, while I left, found a job, got married and had a son. I think I'll find out, and if it is, I'll write and see how James is doing.*

***

Capt. Dunn says out loud, while opening a letter, from Tom Smith, "I can't believe I'm hearing from Tom Smith after all these years.

"My, goodness, Pvt. James Smith is his son and he wants to surprise him with a visit. It'll be good to catch up on old times. I'd get to meet his wife and James' girlfriend."

Capt. Dunn answered the letter immediately.

> Dear Tom,
>
> I think a surprise visit from you, his mother, and his girl is just what the doctor ordered. You know how it is when you first leave home and don't know anyone. Being in a strange town with strange people surely doesn't help either.
>
> James' first leave will be the last weekend in July.
>
> It'll be good to see you again.
>
> Capt. Stanley Dunn

***

What excitement! Tom started making all kinds of plans; *we'll take James to Louisville, and see the sights. Kitty and I will beg off, being tired, and leave James and Susan to themselves. I know James will realize that Susan is more his type to marry, than Melanie will ever be.*

CHAPTER 12

James was thinking, *I've been looking forward to this first weekend pass since I got here. I haven't seen Melanie for such a long time. I just wonder if I will have enough time to tell her everything that has happened and how much I miss her. The bus leaves for Louisville, Kentucky, every hour starting at 1:00 p.m. on Fridays and returns from Louisville every hour starting at 2:00 p.m. I will have to hitchhike or take a Greyhound bus to Lexington, Kentucky. I can't wait to hold Melanie again.*

***

Since the Greyhound bus, going to Lexington, wouldn't leave Louisville until 5:00 p.m., James decided to hitchhike, because he would arrive in Lexington at 6:30 p.m. Then he'd have to find his way to Dream On.

***

As James entered the gate at Dream On he thought, *this is the most beautiful place I've ever seen. It's a picture straight from a painting, with the horses gazing in the meadow. All the trees have a fence around them. I wonder why. I bet it cost a pretty penny to put up all the white board fences. Those fences really set the place off.*

Melanie saw James coming down the lane. She took off her apron, looked in the mirror, and went out the door. James saw Melanie running toward him and he started running toward her. They embraced, kissed, and looked at each other.

Melanie was the first to speak, "James, I'm so glad to see you, and I have so much to tell you. First, I want to know if you would like to attend a dance tomorrow night?" Before James could answer, Melanie continued, "Rowdy, one of the grooms, and he is one of the 40 men I cook for, has invited us to attend a dance in Lexington with him. It would give us a chance to meet some of the other farmers as well as give you a chance to meet the gentlemen I cook for."

James looking at Melanie and seeing the excitement in her eyes, says, "If you really want to go, then we'll go. It should be a lot of fun."

"I really want to go, and I know you and Rowdy will hit it off. Rowdy is our age and he was so bashful when he came to tell me about the dance. He stood there in the doorway with downcast eyes." I asked, "Do you need something, or did you want to tell me something?"

Rowdy answered, "The guys and I were talking, and I was the one that got the short straw. So here I am, not quite knowing what to say but having to tell you."

Impatiently Melanie requested, "Well, come on and tell me."

"There is a dance at the Town Hall in Lexington, Saturday night. We were wondering if you and your parents would like to go with us." With a sigh of relief, Rowdy exclaims, "There, I said it."

"That sounds like fun. However, my intended is coming to see me tomorrow, and I will ask him if he would like to go."

Rowdy started to leave, and with a twinkle in his eye said, "Be sure to make that guy of yours go to the dance. We want to make sure he is good enough for you."

"So, you see, honey," Melanie says, "The guys do look out for me and they appreciate my cooking."

James replies, "Sounds like the dance will be fun. I'd love to go." But James was thinking, *I wonder what my competition looks like.*

CHAPTER 13

Tom, Kitty, and Susan arrived at Ft. Knox a little after 1:00 p.m. They just missed James. After a visit with Capt. Dunn, they were getting ready to leave, Tom asked, "Do you think we could find a place to stay in Louisville until Sunday? Of course the ladies may want to go home."

Susan spoke up in a very loud voice, "I didn't come all this way just to look at the camp and go home. I'm not going home until I see James. If that means I have to stay here by myself, that's okay. I'm sure there is something I can do until James shows up. Better still, why don't we drive to Lexington and see James there?"

Kitty lowered her eyes and said, "Really, Tom. It would be nice to see something of Louisville, and maybe Susan and I could do some shopping."

Tom told the ladies, "I'm sorry, but I don't know the address where the Coxes are working. I'll find the address before we come back again. Kitty, we haven't been away from the farm in a very long time. I think a weekend in Louisville would be great." Turning to Capt. Dunn, Tom says, "Stanley, can you recommend a hotel in Louisville? Don't pick one that charges an arm and a leg, okay?"

Stanley tells them, "There are two hotels right on Fourth Street in downtown Louisville. Neither is very expensive, and they are within walking distance to everything. One is the Seelbach and the other one is the Brown. I'm sure you'd like either one."

CHAPTER 14

After looking at both hotels, and comparing prices, they decided on the Brown Hotel. Tom secured two rooms. One room for Susan, and one room for himself and Kitty. The rooms wee adjoining. Tom and Kitty's room overlooked the corner of Broadway and Fourth Streets.

Susan had the room overlooking Fourth Street. She couldn't help but wonder what all the soldiers were doing in town. *Maybe,* she thought, *there is going to be a parade. Surely not all these soldiers are on leave. I wonder if we will have time to explore the shops across the street and especially the big clothing store on the corner.*

***

Kitty said, "Look, Tom, isn't the church across the street pretty? Can you read the name of it?"

"I'll try." Tom answered, "It's The Warren Memorial Presbyterian Church, and yes, it is pretty. Doesn't it seem out of place with all the businesses around it? Did you notice the drug store? I wonder where all the soldiers are going. They keep going in and out of the church."

Looking thoughtful, Kitty says, "Maybe someone is getting married that the soldiers know."

"Kitty, you will always be an incurable romantic. No one knows that many people. However, you may be right. When we go to eat, we'll ask."

"Tom, Susan and I want to go shopping. You are welcome to come along with us or you can find something else to do." With this, Kitty knocked on the adjoining door.

Susan answered the door and said, "I've been expecting you. I can't wait to see the stores! Shall I meet you in the lobby in about ten minutes?"

Kitty answered, "Sure, we'll see you then."

***

Kitty was enjoying herself, watching Susan try on dresses. She was trying to find something for herself. Everything she liked was either too large or too small. Kitty wasn't going to let her disappointment show.

Susan was getting impatient because she hadn't found a dress she wanted to buy. She was thinking, *I haven't found anything I like. We might as well go on back to the hotel. Hmm, what's this, Gosh, this blue dress with the white trim is pretty. Hope it is my size.* Susan said, "Look at this dress. Isn't it pretty?"

Kitty told her, "It is very pretty and the color will look good on you. Go try it on."

Susan returned shortly in the dress.

Kitty said, "You look like a dream come true in that dress. All the guys will be looking at you, when you wear it."

Susan replied, "I'm going to buy this dress. Now I need to find a pair of shoes, a purse, and a pretty hat to wear." She was thinking, *I'm going to wear my new outfit tomorrow, when we see James. I just know he will be impressed.*

***

While waiting for the girls, in the lobby of the hotel, Tom thought, *the girls are going to be really surprised about the evening I have planned. I can't believe that I am going to see Red Skelton, in person. To think, Louisville has a vaudeville theatre, almost next door to the hotel.*

Kitty walked up to Tom, gave him a small kiss on the cheek, and said, "So what have you been up to?"

Taking her hand, Tom says, "Nothing much, just making reservations for super and seeing if we can see a movie or something after supper."

"Okay, give. I know from the smirk on your face that you are thinking of doing something and you want it to be a surprise."

Tom gives a small laugh and tells his wife, "It will be a surprise, and I don't want to talk about it. Just go put your prettiest clothes on and be pleasantly surprised. Susan, we'll meet in the lobby at 6:30 p.m.

CHAPTER 15

Susan decided to wear the new outfit to dinner with Tom and Kitty. They were waiting for her in the lobby and Tom took one look at Susan and said, "If I were twenty years younger and not married, you'd have my eves for a long time."

Susan blushed and said, "Thank you. Do you think James will like the outfit Sunday?"

Tom answered, "He'd be crazy not to. You sure are a pretty girl."

Kitty spoke up, "I hate to break up this conversation, but I'm hungry. Can we eat now?"

"Of course, honey, I got carried away thinking how James is very foolish to pass over Susan for Melanie."

I refuse to discuss James and Melanie with anyone except James and Melanie." With that, Kitty started toward the elevator.

Catching up with Kitty, Tom says, "Honey, we are going to eat at the restaurant that was cooking the steaks in the window. Then we will go to the National Theatre for a vaudeville show. I'm not going to tell you who the head liner is because you'll be too excited to eat."

***

"The food was exceptionally good. Didn't you think so?" asked Susan.

"I enjoyed it mainly because I didn't have to cook it," laughed Kitty.

"I thought it was good, but I haven't found anyone who can cook better than Kitty. If I ever do then our marriage will be in trouble." Tom winked as he said it, to which Kitty gave him a playful smack on the cheek.

The walk from the restaurant to the National Theatre was a couple of blocks.

Tom looked at the building and said, "Gee, isn't that a work of art? I wonder how long it took them to build it. Just look at the fancy work over the windows and doors. I wonder how they got the tower rooms built without them falling down and how they are anchored so they don't fall now."

As they walked inside the double doors, Kitty's eyes grew big with wonder and she remarked, "Have you ever seen such arches in a building? I wouldn't want the job of cleaning the ceiling or the windows. There must be at least a dozen windows in this hall alone."

Susan laughed and said, "I wondered how long it would take Mrs. Smith to start looking at the buildings as if they were all work, instead of just a pretty building."

Kitty laughed and told Susan, "I can't help it if I notice what needs to be done, and I can tell you they have neglected the care of this building. Why just look at the gaudy red curtains on stage! They not only look old, but in spots they are faded and frayed."

"Well girls, go ahead and pick the housekeeping and building apart. As for me, I came to enjoy the show. And that is that."

Susan made the observation, "I wonder who gets to sit up in the seats along the wall? They don't look very strong to me."

Kitty told her, "Probably someone who is very important, like the mayor, patrons of the arts, or maybe the president, his wife, and the bodyguards, when the president comes to town."

"I wonder if many people come here anymore or if the movies, with the new colors have ruined vaudeville for the general public." Kitty mused.

CHAPTER 16

Walking back to the hotel, Tom asked, "How did you all like the show?"

Before Kitty could answer Susan said enthusiastically, "The dancers were great. I really enjoyed Red Skelton. He is as funny in person as he is on radio. But that singer... wasn't she terrible? I was glad they used the hook on her! I know she needs the money, but I didn't want to hear her sing."

Tom answered, "Well, I think she could sing, but this was just part of the act. Remember when the dancers and the singers were together singing and dancing to several songs? I'm sure one of the singers was the girl they pulled off the stage with the hook?"

Kitty, who had been very quiet said, "I sure hope she was one of the girls. All the girls look like they need a good home-cooked meal. Did you ever see so many undernourished girls in your live?"

"Guess what? I met the nicest soldier during intermission." Susan said, "He was from Ohio and he grew up on a farm. I did find out why all the soldiers are going to the church on the corner. The church heard about the USO, that President Roosevelt is starting for the service men. They wanted to be part of it, so, they have set up the recreational time for the soldiers on leave. The volunteers are there to talk to the soldiers, write letters, and serve coffee and donuts. There is a piano and they have sing-a-longs, as well as dancing." Susan was thinking, *if I could go to school here, I could learn a trade or learn to be a secretary, then I could volunteer at the church and maybe James would come here instead of seeing Melanie.* Susan said, "I think I will ask dad if I can enroll in Spencerian Business School to become a secretary. I could live at the YWCA and go to school. Will you help me convince dad that this is what I need to do? Please, Mr. Smith. Please. Pretty, please."

"With a speech like that, how could I say no?"

Kitty was thinking, *what a dumb idea. We don't know anything about these boys or their families. I wouldn't want my daughter living in a strange town without a friend or family member around. What if she became ill or, worse yet, was taken advantage of by one of these boys? I will definitely tell Janet how I feel. After all, it is their daughter and their decision.*

CHAPTER 17

Tom was the first one awake, Saturday morning. He ran to the window, opened it, stretched, and looked at his wife. He asked, "Are you awake, honey?" When she didn't answer, Tom gently shook her.

"Honey, wake up. We've got a lot of things to do today. I want as much information as possible on the school, the YWCA, and the church. Then I can answer any question that Sam and Janet might have. I think Susan is mature enough that going to school and volunteering at the church will be a good learning experience."

With concern in her voice, Kitty asks, "What if she becomes ill or worse, what if one of these nice young men takes advantage of her and she becomes pregnant? What then? Would she come home, have the baby, and be the talk of the whole county? I don't think Janet could handle it. I doubt Susan could either. You really haven't thought this through."

"Yes, I have." Tom answers defiantly, "That's why I want all the information that I can get. Then I'll know whether to throw my support to Susan or tell her it is a dumb idea."

"That would be wise." Kitty says, as she starts toward the bathroom, "I'll be dressed shortly and after breakfast, we'll start gathering information."

With a smirk and a laugh, Tom says, "I have another surprise for you and Susan."

"Okay, Tom, what is it?" Kitty asks.

"I thought we could visit the J. B. Speed Art Museum, while we're here."

"Great, Tom, I've read about it and I've always wanted to go."

Just then Susan knocked on the adjoining door.

Kitty calls out, "Are you ready to go eat?"

"Yes, I am. Are you?" Susan replied.

"I'll be ready in half an hour. Why don't you meet Mr. Smith in the lobby, and I will join you both shortly?" Kitty tells her.

"That sounds good to me. I may be able to find some information on both the school and the YWCA." Susan answered.

"I'll see you in a minute." Tom responded.

***

"Breakfast wasn't as good as supper last night, did you think so?" Tom asked.

Kitty answered, "I was so hungry. Anything would have tasted good."

"I am so excited about getting the information for dad and mom about the school, I didn't notice the food at all."

"Susan, I must tell you, I am not in favor of you doing this." Kitty tells her, "I, also want you to know, I'll be telling your mother of my concerns."

Susan takes hold of Kitty's hand and pleads, "Please, Mrs. Smith, try to keep an open mind. Try to realize the benefit; I'll receive from this experience."

"I'll try." Kitty answers.

"Good. I can't ask for anything else." Susan was thinking to herself, *I know James will like the idea of my being so close, and I know he'll be coming to see me.*

CHAPTER 18

"My goodness, every building gets prettier," exclaimed Tom, "Just look at the marble corner stones and the canopy over the main door. I wonder how many floors and how many people live here. The YWCA is very pretty."

The girl at the reception desk said, "I'll call Mrs. Schmitt to talk to you. Won't you have a seat?"

Mrs. Schmitt came into the room and Susan stands, holds out her hand and says, "Hi, I'm Susan Brown. This is Mr. and Mrs. Smith. We are from Tennessee and I want to go to school here. But, I need a place to stay. Mr. and Mrs. Smith are gathering information to give to my parents."

Mrs. Schmitt shakes hands with Susan, and Mr. and Mrs. Smith, "It is nice to meet you, Susan, and also, you, Mr. and Mrs. Smith. We have very strict rules. All the young ladies must abide and keep them. They are as follows."

1. Everyone must have written permission from their parents to live here.

2. Everyone must clean their room every day. The bed must be made each morning.

3. Everyone must be in every night, except Saturday night, at 10:00 p.m. Saturday night they must be in by 12:00 a.m.

4. No resident is allowed to have a male visitor in her room at any time.

5. A boy must call at the reception desk to pick up any girl for a date.

6. All girls must act like a lady at all times.

7. All rooms are one bedroom with a bed, night stand, alarm clock, chair, a radio, and a small desk, lamp, and chair.

8. Rent is paid by the week or by the month and is on a sliding scale.

"I hope this has answered your questions. Now would you like to see one of the rooms?"

Tom says, "Before we see the room, would you explain the sliding scale?"

"Of course," Mrs. Smith answers, "Let's say a young lady has a pay check of $20.00 per week. Her rent would be $3.50 per week. If someone was paid $150.00 per month, the rent would be $50.00 per month."

Tom scratches his head and says, "In other words, the rent is based on your income or one third of the gross amount you earn."

Mrs. Schmitt answers, "That is correct. Are there any other questions?"

Tom shakes his head and tells her, "No, let's look at the rooms."

Susan tells them, "This is very nice, and I have a window. I can see what the weather is like."

"Yes, Susan." Mrs. Schmitt tells her, "All the rooms are exactly like this one. They all have a window. Now, let's go to the library, and then you will see the recreation room and the kitchen. While I think of it, please do not let me forget to give you the information on the YWCA."

"I feel a lot better about you staying here," remarked Mrs. Smith.

With laughter in her voice, Susan tells her, "I told you it would be okay, didn't I?"

Mrs. Smith admits, "Yes, you did, but you know what they say, seeing is believing!"

Tom adds his two-cents worth, "I think this is just what the doctor ordered. Thank you, Mrs. Schmitt, for your time and the information. If everything else checks out okay, then I'm sure that Susan will be coming to you for a room."

***

The Spencerian Business School was a few blocks away. Tom Smith was not impressed with the building and let the girls know it. "Are you sure this is where you want to go to school?

There are other schools in the area. I looked at them in the phone book last night."

Susan was infuriated and let it show in her answer, "Mr. Smith, I checked with the desk clerk and the young soldier, I was talking too yesterday. They both said this was the best business school in the area. Sure it is in a building used by other companies and the school is on the second floor, but that doesn't mean the quality of learning is any less. Does it?"

"I guess not." Tom answered, "Let's go see what they have to offer."

CHAPTER 19

Walking into the door, the trio is greeted by a very distinguished gentleman. He extends his hand and says, "Hello, My name is Professor Clark and I am the Dean of Spencerian Business College."

Again, Susan spoke before anyone else could speak, "Nice to meet you, Professor Clark. My name is Susan Brown and this is Mr. and Mrs. Smith. I am just gathering information to give to my parents, when we return to Tennessee. I would like to become a secretary, and I think I would like to attend here. But first, tell me about your school."

"Well, Susan, we do teach all the skills for either office or business employment. Can you type, do you take shorthand, and can you use a mimeograph?"

Susan answers, "I took typing in school and when I graduated, I was typing sixty-five correct words a minute. I didn't take shorthand, but I feel I could learn it without any problems. I can use the mimeograph. I used the one in the school office for the teachers."

Professor Clark looks Susan in the eye and says, "I think we could put you in an accelerated course, and you would get employment within six weeks. However, we do have some requirements."

Kitty was thinking, *Sure you do and it starts with money.*

Handing Susan a brochure of the school's history, Professor Clark states, "The following is a list of requirements that are required of you, not only to enroll, but to remain in the school.

1. Maintain an A or B average.
2. Do not chew gum.
3. Do not cross your legs.
4. Wear your dresses just below the knee.
5. Always wear silk stockings and keep the seams straight.

6. Always wear closed toe shoes and keep them clean and shined.

7. Always wear gloves and a becoming hat.

8. Always act and look like a lady.

9. Most important, wear a smile and have a pleasant personality.

"It sounds as if your school teaches more than just the things to make you a good employee." Tom says.

Professor Clark, with pride in his voice answers, "Yes, we teach everything a girl should know to be a success in the business world. Let me show you around our classrooms. The first is the typing room and we have twenty typewriters. They are used from 8:00 a.m. until 10:00 p.m. every day. Of course on Saturdays, the school closes at 12:00 p.m. The next room is the bookkeeping department. You will learn how to keep two sets of books for any company and how to use and create spread sheets. Now we come to the shorthand room. A lot of people think shorthand is a foreign language. It isn't. But with shorthand you can take down word by word anything that is spoken, no matter how fast a person speaks. These are the basic skills, and after you have mastered these, you may want to go to advanced classes or take a specialized course. Do you have any questions?"

Kitty spoke up, "Yes, I have a very important one. Just how much does the school cost and how long will it be before Susan can expect to be hired by a company?"

"In answer to your question," Professor Clark says, "It would depend on how fast Susan progresses in her studies. Some people graduate in six months, and some graduate in a year. Most students get employment within three weeks of graduating. We are averaging 98% of employment for our students. The students can come back at any time to look for other employment. We have a get-together once a year to see how our students are doing and if they need help with anything. The price would depend on the subjects taken and length of time, Susan would be in school."

Kitty was determined to get some kind of price and said, "This didn't help much as I'm sure Susan's parents and I would like to know if this will cost $500.00 or $5.00 per course."

Professor gave her a look of dismay, "Okay, we really do not like to quote prices until we know what classes the student will be taking. But I will tell you the cost will be between $25.00 and $75.00 per class. I'm sorry I can't be more specific at this time, but until I know exactly what subjects, Susan will be taking, this is the best I can do."

Turning to Susan, Kitty inquires, "Susan, you do have the brochure to take to your parents, don't you?"

Professor Clark extends his hand and says, "It was nice meeting you, and I'm looking forward to having Susan in my school."

As soon as they left the building, Kitty said, "I'm not impressed with Professor Clark or the school. Isn't there another school that will teach the same things?"

Tom says, "We can check the phone book when we get back to the hotel."

Susan stops, stomps her foot, and says, "Really, I would think you would give me a chance to tell you what I think. You both act like you are my parents. I am a person who can make up her own mind. I liked what I saw and what I heard. Also, the school is only four blocks from where I will be living; there will be no streetcar fare, no waiting on a corner for the streetcar, and it is definitely close to my home."

Kitty says, "Well, Susan, it sounds like you have made your mind up."

"Yes, I guess I have." Susan answered. "Now all I have to do is convince dad and mom."

Tom looked at his watch and said, "I think it is time to eat lunch and go to the museum."

CHAPTER 20

Leaving the J. B. Speed Museum and on the steps, Kitty spoke, "I can't believe the length of those tables. Can you imagine feeding that many people at one time?"

Tom tells her, "Sure you can, Kitty. If you remember the Coxes left us for that horse farm, close to Lexington, and Melanie will be cooking or is cooking for forty men. I bet their table is at least that long."

Kitty says, "Well, I definitely wouldn't have some of those statues in my house! The very idea that a nude statue could be art is disgusting. However, the paintings were so life like that I felt I could touch them or move the vases."

Susan had been very quiet until now, "I agree with Mrs. Smith. I wouldn't want my friends to think I looked at those statues, so I'm not going to tell them that we visited this museum."

"You have to admit the building was very impressive. The columns in front reminded me of the pictures, I've seen of some of the Greek buildings in Athens," Tom remarked.

Kitty just looks at Tom and says, "You should have been either an architect or a builder instead of a farmer. The way you look at buildings and decide you could do a better job is just part of your imagination."

CHAPTER 21

Susan was very excited and explained, "Look, we are almost to the hotel, and the church is open to the soldiers again. Let's go in and find out about it."

Tom said with authority, "Okay, but I will not allow you to stay. We are only going to find out the rules for the girls who work there."

As they entered the door, they were met with curious glances. A very well dressed, middle aged lady came to meet them. "Hello, my name is Mrs. Fischer, and I am sorry to tell you, no one is allowed here unless you have your volunteer identification with you."

Tom looked embarrassed and said, "I'm Tom Smith, my wife, Kitty, and a friend of our son's, Susan Brown. Susan is going to persuade her father into letting her move to the YWCA and go to school at Spencerian Business School. She was talking to a young soldier at the National Theatre last evening. She would like to know how she could volunteer. I want to know all the rules, if there are any, so I can tell her parents when we get home."

Mrs. Fischer looked Susan over and asked, "How old are you, Susan?"

"I just turned eighteen last May." Susan replied.

"Have you finished high school?"

"Yes, I finished in the top 10% of my class."

"You must understand that if we let you volunteer, that you cannot date any of the soldiers you meet here. Also, you are not allowed to give out your phone number or where you live to any of the men. We expect you to act and dress the part of a lady. I don't see where that would be a problem, but we are required to tell this to each of our volunteers. Do you have any questions?"

Susan said, "Yes, I do. My friend, James Smith, is stationed at Ft. Knox. Would I be allowed to see him or even date him?

Also, would I be allowed to write to James? Would I have a regular schedule, or could I decide when I want to come in?"

Mrs. Fischer was surprised but answered, "My goodness, you do have some very good questions. I will have to take the question of James up with the board. Volunteering will be at your discretion, but we do like for the girls to let us know when and for how long they will be volunteering. For instance, you may want to volunteer on Friday evening from 7:00 p.m. until 10:00 p.m., or you may just want to volunteer for one evening a month. This is up to you. Our volunteers work with each other to make sure the center is covered every Friday evening and all day Saturday and Sunday. There are very few soldiers here during the week. I would like to take you through our kitchen and the recreation room and let you see how this is ran. I will also give you an application to fill out."

Entering the recreation room, they saw one girl wrapping a present, for a soldier, to be sent home to his girl. Another girl was handing out cookies and pouring coffee. Some of the girls were dancing with the soldiers, and a couple of girls were singing as a soldier played the piano. Tom and Kitty were very impressed. Tom told Mrs. Fischer, "I have never seen anything like this. Do you have a crowd every weekend? Are they always this well behaved?"

"Yes, to both questions." Mrs. Fischer replied, "We get the boys that are homesick or lovesick, and they just need to talk to someone. That is the biggest part of the volunteer's job. Listening and looking at the pictures of home."

Shaking hands with Mrs. Fischer, Tom says, "It was nice meeting you, and thank you so much for taking the time to talk to us. I think Susan will be in touch with you soon."

Outside, Susan couldn't wait to say, "I can't wait to tell James. I know he'll be surprised, and he will also see that I can be anything he wants me to be."

CHAPTER 22

James came into the mess hall to pick Melanie up for the dance. He was thinking, *I am not looking forward to this dance, as I know these guys are going to be looking me over to see if I'm good enough for Melanie. I sure wish it was over.*

Melanie came in dressed in the same dress; she had worn to Mrs. Smith's party. James said, "You are still the prettiest girl in the county, and I love you."

Melanie blushed and said, "I love you too, but we had better be going. I don't want to be late."

***

Rowdy saw them come in and took his girl's hand. They walked over to James and Melanie, and Rowdy introduced himself. "Hi, I'm Rowdy Manship and this is Mary Dearing. Mary, this is our new cook, Melanie Cox, and her intended, James Smith."

James shook Rowdy's hand and said, "It's a pleasure to meet you, and any friend of Melanie's is a friend of mine."

James and Rowdy wandered off to the side to let the girls get acquainted.

James was the first to speak, "Just what brought you to Dream On, Rowdy?"

"Well," Rowdy started speaking, "I was sixteen, and dad didn't think I was taking my responsibilities very seriously. I was born and raised on a horse farm in Maryland. Dad was hoping I would take over the farm when I got older. However, I went to a couple of parties and had a little too much to drink. In a very heated argument I told dad goodbye and left. I'd always heard of Dream On and decided to try to get a job here. They hired me immediately, and I've been here ever since. How did you come to join the army?"

James shifted his weight to his other foot and said, "I was born and raised on my great grandfather's farm in Tennessee. Melanie's family came to work for us six years ago. I think I fell in love with her at first sight. Anyway, dad thought I was getting too serious about her and forbid me to talk or to see her. So, I joined the army and asked Melanie to marry me, when I've saved up some money."

Meanwhile, Melanie and Mary were getting to know each other, and they both knew that a great friendship was about to happen.

"Mary," Melanie asked, "have you lived here all your life?"

Mary answered, "Yes, I was born and raised close to Lexington on a small farm. My mother died when I was born. I was raised by dad's sister, Aunt Grace. Dad and Aunt Grace decided to send me to finishing school in Boston, when I was fourteen. I returned two weeks ago. How did you come here?"

Melanie looks at Mary and tells her, "My folks became share croppers when the dust storms ruined our farm. We were at Tom Smith's farm the last six years. That is where I met James. We were constant companions, and I think I have always loved him."

The music started, and Rowdy came over, took Mary's hand and said, "Excuse us but the first dance belongs to Mary, and I've waited a long time for this dance."

"Melanie," James says while reaching for her hand, "Rowdy is very nice, and I have a feeling he would like to go home. I think his pride keeps him here. Have you ever seen such pretty strawberry blond hair? I think the suntan sets off his blue eyes, don't you?"

Melanie answers, "Yes, and Rowdy has the build of a jockey. He and Mary make a great couple. Mary's coloring, her black hair, and her brown eyes really complement Rowdy. Or should I say Rowdy complements Mary?"

James looks lovingly into Melanie's eyes and says, "Have you ever heard such lively music? And, look how they dance, men in one long line and the women opposite them in another long line."

Melanie exclaims, "Yes, and it does look like fun. This dance is definitely not a waltz, two-step, fox trot, or the polka. I wonder what the dance is called. Did you notice the musical instruments?"

"They all look home-made, but they do make beautiful music." James replies, "I think I would like to learn this dance, wouldn't you?"

With a gasp of excitement and a smile, Melanie replies, "I was hoping you would want to learn. When Rowdy and Mary come back, let's ask them to teach us."

***

"We'll be glad to teach you," Rowdy said, "except I'll have to dance with Melanie and Mary will dance with James, at least for a couple of dances. After that you will be on your own."

Melanie, with her eyes glistening said, "That was the most fun. I'd like to come to all the dances."

"I really enjoyed the dance too. I would like to come as often as I can," James replied, "but I have to start back to camp. Sure hope I can find a ride to Louisville."

Rowdy thinks a minute and says, "You know what? Mary's father is here, and I will ask him if Mary can go with me to take you to Louisville. If Melanie's parents agree, we'll take her along. Would that be okay?"

"Great! James exclaimed, "It would give me a little extra time with the girl of my dreams."

***

What a trip to Louisville! The friendship between the four young people was sealed on the trip.

James states, "You know, I've been telling some of the guys in my unit about Melanie and me planning to get married. Some of the guys are married and their wives work on the base while some of the other wives work in the nearby towns. What would you say, Melanie, if we got married now, and you could go with me?"

Before Melanie could answer, Rowdy said, "Absolutely not. Melanie is the best cook we have had in a long time, and the guys won't give her up even for you."

Melanie answers, "James, you know that dad signed a contract for himself, mother, and me to work at Dream On for the next year at least. We could get married, but I have to fulfill the commitment for dad."

"What if you got a substitute to finish your contact?" Mary asked.

Melanie starts twisting her hair and says, "That might work, but who would I get?"

"What about me?" asked Mary laughing, "You see, Aunt Grace does everything in the house including the garden, and I sit around looking pretty. Anyway, if I took your place I could keep a close eye on Rowdy."

"I would still have to get dad's approval, but I'm sure he will agree."

James took Melanie in his arms and gave her a final, long kiss before boarding the bus.

Rowdy, Mary, and Melanie watched the bus pull away, taking James back to camp. They got in the car and started towards home.

***

Melanie slept on the way home but was having dreams about her wedding and what the future would hold for her and James.

Mary slept, content knowing she would be with Rowdy every day and someday they would be getting married.

CHAPTER 23

James slept soundly, dreaming of the future with Melanie by his side. Just as his dream started to include the future children, James was awakened by the phone ringing.

The dispatcher said, "Pvt. James Smith, you have visitors waiting to see you."

Still groggy from sleep, James asks, "Who are they?"

"It's your mother, father, and your girlfriend." The dispatcher answered.

James shakes his head and says, "Okay, I'll be right up."

I wonder why mom and dad brought Susan. James thought, *And to let the dispatcher think she was his girl, that was an insult to injury. It doesn't matter; I'm going to tell them, I'm going to marry Melanie and take her with me wherever I'm stationed. I really needed the walk this morning to clear my head and to decide on my future with Melanie.*

***

Mrs. Smith reached her son first. James kissed and hugged his mother, shook his father's hand, and looked at Susan. Then James spoke, "Susan, it is nice of you to come to see me. However, you wasted a trip, because I love Melanie, and I'm going to marry her as soon as possible. The only way you and I can be friends is if you accept Melanie as your equal and treat her with respect. The other thing is I do not want you to write, call, or visit me. You can correspond with Melanie, and she will let you know how we are doing. Do you understand?"

Susan was devastated but said, "James, I was trying to bring a little sunshine into the dreary life of my favorite soldier. However, whatever you say, I'll try to do. Yes, I'll treat Melanie as an equal. I'd do anything to please you. By the way, I'm going to be living at the YWCA in Louisville, while I go to business school. I hope you will stop to see me on your way to see Melanie."

Susan thought, *I'm not about to give James up without a fight. Just because I promised him I would treat Melanie as an equal, doesn't mean that I can't put a few stumbling blocks in the way. Maybe just one of the blocks will send James back to me.*

Mr. Smith realized, *James loves Melanie the same way I loved Kitty all those years ago. By gum, she still loves me! She may love me even more than she did when we were courting.*

Mrs. Smith was thinking, *I'll have to get in touch with Mrs. Cox. We have a mountain of things to do before the wedding. I hope Susan means what she said about becoming friends with Melanie; otherwise, she will cause trouble.*

CHAPTER 24

As soon as the car stopped in the driveway, Susan told the Smiths, "Thanks for a lovely weekend and I'll let you know if I need your help to convince mom and dad to let me move to Louisville."

Susan went immediately to the barn to see her father, "Dad, I would like to move to Louisville. I know it is a long way from here but I can go to school and become a secretary. I've heard you talk about Hitler and how he wants to rule the world. Well, if the U.S. goes to war, my being here as a lady won't help. Knowing a trade will help. Won't you say yes and help me convince mom that this is the right thing to do?"

"What's your real reason for wanting to go to school in Louisville? I know that Louisville is a lot closer to Fr. Knox than this is. You would be closer to James, and I'm going to tell you right now, leave James and Melanie alone! I've seen the way James looks at Melanie and the way Melanie looks at James. If you did succeed in getting James to marry you, you'd be buying yourself a lot of unhappiness. James would be a good husband and father, but his heart will always belong to Melanie. Do you think you could live with James knowing that he was yours in marriage only, and you would always be second to Melanie? Think about it, and we'll talk again, about this, in a few days." With this said, Mr. Brown turned and walked away towards the house.

Susan didn't expect this from her dad. She did expect her mother to feel this way, but not dad. Dad always did what she wanted. Susan wondered, *Am I losing my touch with the men in my life? First it was James, and now dad? Well, I've got to convince them to let me go to Louisville.* Then it occurred to Susan, *I'll get mom to invite the Smiths over and then I'll direct the conversation toward our visit in Louisville. The Smiths will tell my parents about the school, living arrangements, and the museum.*

Susan's heart and spirits were on cloud nine as she walked towards the house. She would tell her mother of the trip to Louisville. Susan knew she would enjoy hearing about the things she had done and the things she had seen.

***

Janet Brown had been apprehensive about Susan going to Louisville with the Smiths. Now, looking out the window of the kitchen, she was even more uneasy. Susan was almost skipping from the barn with excitement. Janet thought, *This can't be good. Susan is up to something and she wants me to be her ally. Please, God, give me the wisdom to do what is right and the strength to enforce the decision.*

"Hi, mom," Susan said as she embraced her mother. "You can't believe the sights or the excitements of a town like Louisville. I'd love for you to invite the Smiths over. Then we can tell you about everything we did. How about it? Will you? Please."

How could she refuse, thought Janet? So Janet said, "Go ask the Smiths to come to supper Wednesday evening about 6:00 p.m."

That sure was easy. Susan thought. Kissing her mother on the cheek, she left for the Smiths' home.

Susan knew Mr. Smith was on her side, but was uncertain how Mrs. Smith felt.

Well, thought Susan, *I can only hope Mrs. Smith will help mom and dad decide to let me move.*

***

Mrs. Smith greeted Susan with a hug and said, "How nice of you to stop by. I just took some cookies from the oven. Would you like some?"

"Yes. I would." Susan replied.

Sitting down at the kitchen table with their coffee and cookies, Susan and Mrs. Smith began talking about the trip to Louisville.

The more they talked and reminisced about the trip, the more excited Susan became. Finally Susan said, "Mom would like for you and Mr. Smith to come to supper, Wednesday about 6:00 p.m. I hope you can make it. I hope you can come."

"Of course we can." Mrs. Smith exclaimed, "Would you like for us to bring the brochures of the school and the YWCA with us?"

Susan lowered her eyes and said, "Please try to convince mom and dad that this is something I really want to do. Guess what, I just realized, I want to do this for myself. It really has nothing to do with James."

With a sigh of relief, Mrs. Smith says, "Now I'm convinced the move will be good for you."

Susan rose to leave, gave Mrs. Smith a hug, and said, "I'll see you Wednesday."

CHAPTER 25

Melanie was walking very slowly from the mail box. The letter in her hand held very disturbing news.

Dear Melanie,

It was great to see you and hold you even if it was for just a short time. I like Rowdy and Mary, a lot. The dance was fun, and you were so pretty, the prettiest girl at the dance.

I had some surprise visitors Sunday afternoon. Mom, dad, and Susan came to see me. Susan wants to move to Louisville, go to school, and volunteer at a church. The church provides recreation for service men. But don't worry; the church forbids their volunteers to date any service man. Besides, my heart belongs to a beautiful girl who lives in Lexington, Kentucky. I think her name is Melanie. I met this girl on my father's farm.

I told mom and dad about our plans to marry soon, so you could go with me when I'm transferred. I hope you will set the date real soon. I love you so much, and we will have a wonderful life together.

Love always,

James

P.S. Write soon.

What was Susan thinking? Could she actually think by being in Louisville, she would see James every time he came to see me? thought Melanie. *Well, I guess I'll have to make friends with Susan just to keep an eye on her, if nothing else. Please, God give me the strength and wisdom to deal with Susan.*

***

Rowdy walked into the mess hall, took one look at Melanie, and said, "Okay, what is the matter? You look like you just saw a ghost."

Melanie tells Rowdy, "I got a letter from James. Susan, a childhood friend of James, is moving to Louisville. I know she is planning on seeing James each time he comes through Louisville. Everyone thought James and Susan would marry. I'm not sure how to handle this."

For a second Rowdy was quiet. Then he said, "Mary and I will pick James up in Louisville. We'll even bring Susan here and take her to the dance. After all, there are several guys, without girlfriends, and we'll see they all get to meet Susan."

Melanie looks at Rowdy with gratitude showing in her eyes and says, "Okay, Rowdy, it sounds great, but what if James is one of the guys that takes a shine to her? I don't think I could live without James."

"Don't worry," Rowdy says, "James would have taken a shine to her way before this if he had wanted to, but he chose you. Everything will be okay."

Melanie says, "I'll write and tell James to be sure to give Susan my phone number, so we can make plans. Thank you, for both the advice and for being my friend."

***

Melanie knew that Susan always received what she wanted from her mother and dad. Even with Rowdy's reassuring words, Melanie was still unsure. *Well,* she thought, *I'll have to be more beautiful, charming, and supportive to James.*

John came in the mess hall with a big grin on his face and said, "Hi, young lady. Is James going to be here this weekend?"

Melanie answered, "I'm not sure, but I'm hoping he will. Can I ask you a question?"

I'm not sure I can answer it, but I'll try." John said.

Melanie starts pacing the floor and twisting her hair, "Susan, a childhood friend of James, is moving to Louisville. I'm sure she is trying to get James to forget me, and I'm not sure I'm strong enough to keep James from her clutches. Rowdy said he and

Mary would pick James and Susan up in Louisville, bring them here, and hopefully Susan would meet someone at the dance. What would you do?"

John thinks for a minute and then says, "I think Rowdy is right. Remember you can lead a horse to water, but you can't make him drink. I can see why you're concerned, but I don't think you have a thing to worry about. The way James looks at you says that you are the only girl for him, regardless of who tries to take him away."

"Thanks John," Melanie replies, "You have helped me a lot, and since you and Rowdy said almost the same thing, I feel much better."

Melanie thought, *Maybe mom could make me a new dress for the first time Susan is with us.*

CHAPTER 26

Why is the time going so slow? thought Susan as she helped her mother fix supper for the Smiths? *Just one more hour. I hope the Smiths can convince mom and dad to let me go. Just think, I'll see James every time he has leave. Eventually, James will see that I'm more his type than Melanie ever was.*

Meanwhile, Mrs. Brown was praying under her breath, *please, God, help me make the right decision on Susan wanting to move to Louisville. Please do not let Susan influence James into breaking up with Melanie. Not my will, but yours be done. I ask this in the name of the Father, the Son, and the Holy Ghost.*

***

"Hello and welcome neighbor." Sam Brown said as he answered the door for the Smiths.

"Hi." Tom answered, "I think fall has set in. I'm dreading winter."

Kitty interrupted and said, "Are Susan and Janet in the kitchen?"

Sam replied, "Yes, they are. Why don't you join them, as I want to talk business with Tom."

As soon as Kitty left the room, Sam turned to Tom and said, "Let's sit down and discuss the school Susan wants to go to."

Tom run his hand through his hair, shakes his head and says, "I was hoping to discuss that with the ladies present, but since you brought it up, I'll tell you. I was very hesitant at first, but we got to talk to the director of studies, and I quickly changed my mind. The students are placed in jobs, some before graduation and some after graduation. All students can return at anytime for additional employment help.

"We then went to the YWCA and likewise we were given a tour, and believe me, the rules of the house are even stricter than our rules. So, I see no problem with her staying there as they have twenty-four hour supervision.

"And last, but not least, and the reason I feel Susan really wants to stay is the Warren Presbyterian Church. The church is trying to qualify for a USO certification. This is the program that President Roosevelt is sponsoring for the service men. The girls are not allowed to have outside contact with any of the service men. Susan has asked permission to see James, and the lady in charge told her, she would bring this to the attention of the board. The board's decision would be final."

"I brought brochures on the school and the YWCA. You and Janet can look them over before you make your decision. However, I think it would be a great experience, a safe environment, and an education she could use the rest of her life."

CHAPTER 27

As soon as Kitty entered the kitchen, Susan said, "Hello, Mrs. Smith. I was just telling my mother about the school. Maybe you would like to continue what I started."

"I think I would," Mrs. Smith answered, "First, let me say I really do not approve of young girls leaving home for selfish reasons. However, I do realize Susan's moving to Louisville would be a great opportunity, and after interviewing the school, YWCA, and the Warren Presbyterian Church, Susan would have the support, rules, and discipline of adults, and she would be very safe. I think if I were Susan's age, I would like to live in Louisville, go to school, and volunteer at the Church. Those boys are so lonely, and the girls are not allowed to date the servicemen or see them outside of the church. Susan did ask about seeing James, and Mrs. Fischer told her she would bring it up at the director's meeting. Mrs. Fischer also told Susan that the decision would be final and rules would be enforced.

"Susan and Tom both brought brochures for you and Sam to look over, so you can make a wise decision. I do think it is a great opportunity for Susan."

Mrs. Brown says, "I do feel better about Susan's request. I'll make a decision after I've read the brochures and discussed it with Sam. Supper is ready to put on the table. Susan, go tell the men to wash up."

By the time supper was over, both Janet and Sam were agreed that Susan going to Louisville would be a great experience.

Janet said, "Susan, I think your moving to Louisville would be a great opportunity, so if Sam agrees you can start packing."

Sam with a forlorn look says, "I think so too, but I hate to see my little girl go so far away. Anyway, it'll give us an excuse to make the trip more often."

"I'm so excited, I feel like a school girl myself," exclaimed Mrs. Smith. "Maybe the four of us could go together to help Susan get started. How about it, Tom?"

Tom started counting on his fingers, looked up at his wife and said, "I've already started thinking of when we could go. Of course, we have to think of James and his plans with Melanie. Maybe we could all go to the dance, James was telling us about."

Sam added, "I'll call the school and the YWCA in the morning."

Susan said, "I knew you would let me go, and I'll do my best to make you very proud of me." Her thoughts are, *including you, James. After all, you want a wife who is polished and an asset to the community, not a cook for a bunch of farm hands.* "If you don't mind, I think I'll go to my room. I want to write to James and tell him the good news."

Mrs. Brown says, "You go ahead, and we'll make plans to take you to your new home."

CHAPTER 28

Moving day came all too soon for Janet Brown, and she was thinking, *it sure will be lonely here without Susan. But the time has come for her to leave the nest. I wish we lived closer to Louisville. Please, God, look out for my daughter and please keep her safe from harm. I ask this in Jesus' name. Well, there's no use sitting here wishing; I've got things to do and the Smiths will be here at any minute.*

The Smiths arrived, and Susan went to meet them.

Opening the door, Mrs. Smith looked at Susan and asked, "Good morning, Susan, and how did you sleep last night?"

Greeting Mrs. Smith with a hug, Susan said, "Hello, and how did you know I didn't sleep. I'm so excited and anxious to start my new adventure."

Sam Brown shook hands with Mr. Smith and said, "Shall we take my car? I think it is a little larger."

"Okay by me, only let's get started." Tom said.

***

As soon as Tom and Kitty were settled into their room at the Brown Hotel, Tom called Captain Dunn, "Hello, Dunn, Tom Smith here."

"Hello, Tom. I take it you are back in Louisville."

"Yes we are and I would like to leave a message for James, if I may."

"Of course, but you'll have to hurry as James has the weekend off."

"Tell James we are in Louisville and will meet the next bus from Ft. Know."

"Will do. Tell Kitty hello for me."

***

"I'm glad I caught you." Capt. Dunn says as he walks into the barracks where James is staying. "Your father called and they are in Louisville. He said to tell you they would meet the next bus from here."

James showed the anxiety in his voice, when he said, "I hope they aren't still trying to cause Melanie and me trouble."

Capt. Dunn says, "Son, just take everything with a grain of salt. Include Susan in your weekends, and pray she finds someone she likes better than you."

"I think I can do that, and I hope Melanie understands." James replies.

"Good luck, son." And with that Capt. Dunn left the barracks.

It's too late to call Rowdy. They have already left to pick me up in Louisville. Well, I guess I'll go and face the music! James thought as he picked up his hat and walked out the door.

CHAPTER 29

As Melanie, Mary and Rowdy entered the bus station, Melanie exclaimed, "Look, there are the Browns, Smiths, and of course Susan."

"Now, now, don't get upset." Rowdy says, "You knew Susan was moving to Louisville. The Browns and Smiths wouldn't let her move without coming to get her settled. I tell you, let's go over and invite the whole group to the dance tonight. They could follow us back to the farm."

Mary remarked, "I think it is a grand idea. Better to have the enemy where you can keep an eye on them. Right, Melanie?"

Melanie, looking at the group thought, *Am I going to have to put up with Susan every weekend?* She said instead, "I think it's a good idea."

Reaching the group first, Melanie says, "What a pleasant surprise. I would like to introduce you to my friends, Rowdy Manship and Mary Dearing. Rowdy and Mary, this is Susan Brown, her parents, Mr. and Mrs. Brown, and these are James' parents, Mr. and Mrs. Smith."

Before they could start a conversation, the bus pulled in and all eyes were watching for James.

James got off the bus, went immediately to Melanie, hugged, and kissed her. Poor Susan was beside herself as she was hoping James would acknowledge her first. However, James then hugged his mother, shook hands with his father, the Browns, and said to Susan, "I hope your stay in Louisville is enjoyable and you make lots of friends. Melanie and I are busy making our wedding plans and won't have time to entertain you."

Before Susan could answer, Melanie said, "I think it would be great if everyone followed us to Lexington and went to the dance with us tonight. Don't you?"

The last thing I want is having Susan tag along. James thought, but he said, "Sure the more the merrier."

Rowdy said, "Okay, it's settled then. Susan, you can ride with us, that is if your parents approve, and the parents can follow us."

Walking out of the bus station, Sam asked, "Where are you parked? I'm parked on Fifth Street and my car is a '38 Model T Ford."

"Good." Rowdy answered, "I'm parked on fifth also."

Mrs. Smith was very pleased and said, "This will give us a chance to discuss the wedding and I'm hoping, Janet, that you will offer advice.

Susan thought to herself, *at least I'll be in the same car with James. He'll see how much better educated I am than these country bumpkins.*

CHAPTER 30

Rowdy told Susan, "You will sit the first dance out as everyone has a partner for the first dance. After that, because you are new, there won't be any time for you to sit down."

Susan replied, "I'm really not interested in meeting anyone. Since I understand this is a different dance than what I am used to, I doubt that I will enjoy it one bit."

With anger showing in his voice, James replied, "Susan, don't try to make the dance miserable for everyone. After all, God made all these people the same as he did you. I expect you to dance with whoever asks you and let me tell you right now, it isn't going to be me. My dances all belong to Melanie."

Susan's eyes were flashing and there was an edge to her voice when she replied, "Well in that case, *James*, if I want to dance, I will, if not, I won't." and she started to stomp off, but Melanie stopped her.

Before James could answer, Melanie said, "Susan, I know this is different from what you are used to. We have different customs. Mary and I would like to help you adjust, if you are going to be living in Louisville. Back in Tennessee, you were the belle of the ball. Here you will be just one of the girls. There isn't much class distinction between the rich and the poor."

Still with an edge to her voice, Susan says, "Melanie, it is sweet of you and Mary to offer, but I will probably be too busy to accept your offer except on weekends."

Smiling at Susan, Melanie replies, "Then we shall look forward to the weekends."

***

Watching the people dance and listening to the music, Susan thought, *I've never heard music like this and everyone is so nice.*

Mom and dad are enjoying themselves, as are the Smiths. I wonder if all these people are farm hands.

Walking over to Mary, Susan said, "See the guy standing by the band, the tall one. His hair is so wavy and the same color as mine."

Mary answered with a question to her answer, "Yes?"

"Well, if he isn't married or spoken for, I'd like to dance with him."

"Susan, I'll check with Rowdy and let you know."

In a few minutes, Rowdy came over and said, "Susan, there is a gentleman here that wants to meet you, but he is shy. See the tall guy standing next to the band? That is Jeff Spencer. His family owns Whirl-a-Way farms. If you would be willing to meet him, I'll walk you over."

"Gee, Rowdy, I was telling Mary how handsome I think he is. Let's go!"

When they reach Jeff, Rowdy says, "Jeff Spencer, I would like you to meet Miss Susan Brown from Tennessee. Susan, this is Jeff Spencer from Lexington."

From that moment on, there wasn't anyone in the room for either Jeff or Susan, except each other. They danced every dance with each other and got to know each other between dances.

James said to Melanie, "Looks like Susan has found someone to occupy her time."

Melanie answered, "It does, doesn't it? I'm so glad." *Maybe she'll give up on James and quit trying to cause trouble,* she thought.

When the dance ended, the Browns and Smiths said "Goodbye, we'll see you next time. That was a lot of fun."

Mr. Brown said, "Susan, tell them bye and come back with us. I'm sure they'll stop by tomorrow before James leaves for camp."

"Of course we will, but Susan is welcome to stay with me if she wants to." Melanie said.

With eyes dancing, Susan asks, "Could I, dad?"

Mr. Brown hesitated, but Mrs. Brown said, "I think that would be lovely, and it will give Mary and Melanie more time to get to know you."

""Then it's settled. We'll see you tomorrow." Mr. Brown remarked.

Mrs. Smith asked, "James, are you coming with us, or are you staying here?"

To which James answered, "Mom, I will stay in the bunk house with Rowdy. Melanie and I have things to talk about, and we have so little time together."

Mrs. Smith replied, "Until tomorrow. I love you, son."

Mr. Smith and Mr. Brown shook hands all around, and then they left.

CHAPTER 31

The girls were ready for bed when Melanie said, "James and I will be married here, on the lawn of the big house."

Susan says, "I really thought you would be married at the Smith's. That is where you met, grew up, and fell in love."

"Yes, Susan," Melanie replied, "but we both live here and have our friends here. Of course anyone is welcome to come, that would like to."

Mary chimed in, "Susan you haven't seen a celebration until you attend our weddings."

With this, Susan answered. "We roast a pig with all the trimmings. There are all kinds of prepared vegetables, salads, and desserts. An orchestra is hired to play lovely songs throughout dinner with dancing afterward. There'll be aunts, uncles, cousins on both sides of James' families and friends of both Melanie and James."

"It sounds wonderful." Melanie says, "But, it would mean the wedding would be three days after James starts his 30 day leave. No, the wedding will be here."

"Besides, Susan," Mary spoke up, "we do almost the same things at our weddings. Instead of chamber music, we have a hoe down. I have attended weddings both ways. Believe me, I'd rather go to a wedding with a hoe down band, than an orchestra. Hoe downs are more fun."

"Did you go to school someplace besides here, Mary?" asked Susan.

"Yes," Mary answered, "I attended finishing school in Boston, Massachusetts; I started attending the school, when I was fourteen."

"You were lucky. Mom and dad told me, I could learn everything I needed to know from mom." Susan says, with downcast eyes and twisting her hands.

Mary reaches over and touches Susan's hands, "You did learn everything you need to know from your mother. Unfortunately my mother died when I was born. Aunt Grace felt I needed to learn things, she couldn't teach me."

With regret in her voice and a tear in her eye, Susan says, "I'm so sorry, Mary. I just don't know what I would do without my mother."

Melanie said, "Mary has become my dearest friend. In fact, Mary has agreed to be my maid of honor. Rowdy agreed to be James' best man. It will be a simple ceremony with just the parents and a few special friends. However, the reception will be large, noisy, and fun. As one of James' and his parents' closest friends, we wouldn't think of excluding you."

Mary says, "Do you realize we have talked most of the night? We'd better go to sleep or we won't make it to church tomorrow... this morning."

***

James asked, "What do you think of Susan, Rowdy?"

"Susan, for all her show of acceptance," replies Rowdy, "is going to cause trouble for you and Melanie. She is determined to marry you."

"Maybe not, Rowdy," James answers. "She is going to school and doing volunteer work. Surely, she'll meet someone and fall in love with him. I don't think she loves me, but is in love with the thought of being in love."

Shaking his head, Rowdy says, "You may be right. I sure hope so."

CHAPTER 32

Melanie was walking very slowly to the mail box. Her heart was breaking, and she knew that James would be upset when he received her letter. This is all James' fault.

Melanie turned the letter over and over in her hand while thinking; *He lied to me and betrayed my trust. I should have told my mother about the letter I received from Susan. But, I was so ashamed, and I didn't want to believe her.*

I know, both Susan's and James' parents wanted them to marry, but I was the girl that James chose. I hope I can be a lady during the wedding ceremony between Susan and James. I really do not feel that James or I have a choice except for him to marry Susan. I couldn't marry James knowing Susan is pregnant. I know James would want to do the right thing and give the baby a name. I love James so much and was looking forward to being his wife and having his children.

Melanie took Susan's letter from her pocket and reread it again for the fourth time.

Dear Melanie,

I know that you and James are planning your wedding. However, I think you should know, James and I have been intimate on several occasions. We didn't want to hurt you and thought we were careful not to have anything happen. Unfortunately, the last time we were intimate, was about two months ago. I think I'm pregnant. I haven't told James yet because he doesn't want to hear from me. You should also know that I have been writing to James ever since he went into the army.

James told me that he was going to marry you and take you with him to his next assignment.

Please let me know how you are going to handle this. I know this will be extremely hard for both you and James.

Yours truly,
Susan

***

James walked anxiously to mail call thinking, *I haven't heard from Melanie for a couple of days. I sure hope everything is okay and I get a letter from her today.*

"Private James Smith." The mail clerk called out.

James' heart was in his mouth as he took the letter from the mail clerk.

Great, James thought, *I finally got a letter from Melanie.*

James' joy was short-lived. With a yell that could be heard in the next county James said, "How could Susan tell such a lie? What was she thinking? Is she that determined to marry me, even though she knows I will always love Melanie? What can I do? What should I do? Whom should I confide in? Please, please, help me Lord!"

Capt. Dunn saw how much distress James was in and came over to speak to him. "James, is something the matter? Can I help? Sometimes it helps to talk about the thing that is brothering you."

"Thank you Capt. Dunn." James said, as he handed Melanie's letter to him.

Capt. Dunn read the letter, handed it back to James and said, "This isn't so bad, but I must ask, did you have relations with Susan?"

"No, absolutely not," answered James, "We wrestled when we were kids, but I haven't touched her since mom and dad said we were too old to wrestle with each other. I guess I must have been about ten years old and Susan was about eight.

"Okay, the first thing is to enlist reinforcements." Capt. Dunn said, "Call your mother; tell her about the letter to Melanie from Susan. Then call Melanie and assure her that Susan is up to her old tricks and you are taking care of it. You may have to tell Melanie that you called your mother, but that's all right. If for some reason Melanie will not talk to you, don't worry, have your mother call her. Let me know what happens and if there is anything I can do."

"Thanks for talking to me." I'm going to call mom now." James saluted Capt. Dunn and walked away.

CHAPTER 33

As soon as Mrs. Smith heard James' voice, she knew something was very wrong. "What's the problem, son?" Is Melanie ill or did she call off the wedding? Tell me what the problem is and I'll do what I can to correct it."

"Mom, you know that I have never told you a lie, have I?"

"No, son, you've always told the truth. Now let's have it. What is the problem? I can't help, if I don't know what it is."

"Mom, this is so hard for me to tell you, but here it is. I received a letter from Melanie today. I hadn't heard from her for a couple of days and I knew something was wrong. I wasn't sure what. Melanie received a letter from Susan.

"Susan," James had to stop and swallow hard before he could proceed, "Told Melanie that she and I had been intimate and that Susan is expecting. Without asking me, Melanie believed Susan and told me, in her letter, to marry Susan. Please help me, mom. I've been saving myself for the girl I marry ever since I was a young boy, so if Susan is pregnant... it isn't mine."

Mrs. Smith let out a sigh and says, "Just stay calm. You aren't the first boy to be falsely accused, and you won't be the last. I'll get in touch with Mrs. Brown and see if Susan has told her about the baby. In the meanwhile, you get in touch with Melanie and tell her, we are working on the problem. I bet that Melanie has not told her mother. Otherwise, you wouldn't have gotten the letter. I've got to run, I love and you'll hear from me shortly."

"I love you, too. I'll call Melanie." James hangs the phone up and walks over to his bunk. *I need to think what I'm going to say, before I call Melanie. How do I explain such an out and out lie. Please help me, Lord.*

CHAPTER 34

The men knew as soon as they came into the mess hall that something was wrong. They could see that Melanie had been crying. However, breakfast wasn't any different than any of the other meals except there was little conversation.

John has always had a soft spot for Melanie and came back to the mess hall the first chance he got. After he got a cup of coffee, he sat down at the table and said, "Okay, little lady, what is the problem?"

Melanie answered, "Oh, John, it is so horrible. I don't want to talk about it."

"How am I going to help you, if you don't tell me?" John answered.

Twisting her hair, Melanie says, "Okay, but please don't tell anyone else. Promise?"

"Yes, I promise." John agrees reluctantly.

Melanie hands him the letter from Susan. "I received this letter a few days ago from Susan. Please read it."

John read the letter and said, "I'm going to tell you a story about someone I was very close to. A long time ago, this fellow was engaged to a wonderful girl. Another girl wrote the first girl the same type of letter. Well, the first girl broke off the engagement, so the guy could marry the expectant mother. The girl wasn't pregnant after all, and so she ruined the boy's, the girl's, and her own life because she was selfish, petty, and mean. Just do me a favor and check around. Make sure Susan is pregnant."

Melanie wanted to know more about the three people and asked, "What happened to the three people involved?"

John blushed and said, "The boy was me. I married the girl who claimed to be pregnant. The love of my life wouldn't hear of anything else. My love became an old maid. My wife did have my child, three years after our marriage. By then, I couldn't find work, so I thought it would be better to go where the work was and send for my wife and child after I got settled. It has never happened. My daughter would be about your age. I still regret not marrying my love and forgetting the woman I married."

"Thanks a million, John, you have given me hope and the first thing I'm going to do is talk to James."

John rose from the table, took his cup to the sink, rinsed it, and started for the door, "Talking to James is the right thing to do. Let me know if I can do anything."

CHAPTER 35

Mrs. Cox was shocked when she saw Melanie. Melanie's eyes still showed signs of crying. Mrs. Cox took Melanie in her arms and asked, "What is wrong, dear?"

Snuggling closer to her mother, Melanie says, "Oh, mom, you have no idea. I received this letter from Susan a few days ago, and I couldn't bring myself to either show the letter or discuss it. John stopped in for coffee this morning. He made me see I needed you to advise me. So, please read the letter and then give me your opinion."

"Well, I see Susan isn't going to give up very easily." Mrs. Cox said, after she had reread the letter the second time. "Have you talked to James?"

"No, mom, I haven't, but I did write him a letter telling him to marry Susan."

Standing back and looking at Melanie, Mrs. Cox says, "Why did you do such a foolish thing?"

Melanie answers, "Because I was hurt, disappointed, and shocked. How could James proclaim his love for me and be intimate with Susan. There is the baby to consider. You know how people talk, and the baby would have to live with the disgrace the rest of his or her life."

With anger in her voice, Mrs. Cox says, "Now you listen to me young lady! There isn't any proof of James ever having been intimate with Susan, and there definitely is no proof there is going to be a baby. I want you to get on the phone and call James. Ask James all, and I do mean all, the questions that you have regarding Susan and his relationship with her."

Melanie starts for the door, turns, gives her mother a hug and tells her, "Yes, mom, I will as soon as I get to my room."

***

As Melanie entered her room, the phone was ringing. She answers, "Hello."

"Hi, hon." James says, "I want you to know I love you more than life itself. I have never been intimate with Susan. I have no idea if she is pregnant or not, but I do know if she is, the baby isn't mine. I do hope you believe me because it's true."

Melanie is twisting her hair and tells him, "I'm sorry I wrote the letter without talking to you first. I was so shocked, hurt, and disappointed. I thought the honorable thing to do would be for you to marry her. I wasn't thinking straight. Can you forgive me?"

James tells her, "Honey, there is nothing to forgive. Mom is calling Susan's mother, and they will get to the bottom of Susan's lie."

Melanie says, "As soon as you hear anything, please call me. I love you."

James lowers his voice and coos into the phone, "I love you and call me if you hear anything. By the way, don't you dare cancel any of the wedding plans. I only want to be your husband and the father of our children. Bye for now, darling, I love you."

CHAPTER 36

The phone rang and Mrs. Brown answered, "Hello."

"Hello, Janet. This is Kitty Smith. How are you?"

Puzzled as to why Kitty has called her, Janet Brown answers, "I'm fine and how are you?"

"I'm fine but have you heard from Susan?" Kitty asked.

Even more puzzled, Janet says, "Not since last week. Why? What is the trouble?"

Kitty takes a big breath and says a short prayer, *Please God help me tell Janet. I ask this in the name of Jesus, not my will but thine be done.* "I really don't know how to tell you, but I don't have a choice. I hope our friendship can withstand this news."

Janet is getting very aggravated and says, "Really, Kitty. We have been friends too long to have anything hurt our friendship. So whatever you need to say… just say it!"

Kitty tells her, "Well, here goes, I got a phone call from James this afternoon and he was very upset. James had received a letter from Melanie. It seems that Susan wrote a letter to Melanie. The letter informed Melanie of the intimacy between James and Susan. Susan thinks she is pregnant. James told me that Susan had made this up and if she is pregnant it definitely wasn't his."

"I knew it!" exclaims Janet, "I knew Susan was up to no good, when she insisted on moving to Louisville. I did hope she would meet someone. Anyway, I think we should take Susan to a doctor. That would mean another trip to Louisville. Are you up to it?"

"I was hoping you would want Susan to go to the doctor." Kitty says, "Shall we plan on going to Louisville, next week?"

Janet hesitates before answering, "That sounds good except I would like to know if I'm going to be a grandmother or not as soon as possible. We will have to tell our husbands. They'll have a hard time getting away right now."

Kitty thinks a minute and says, "Let's tell them Susan called and is very homesick. Since they are tied up with the harvest, we can go by ourselves. What do you think?"

Janet agrees, "Perfect. I'll call Susan and tell her to expect us. I'll not tell her why. We'll give her enough rope to hang herself."

CHAPTER 37

Neither of the ladies had much to say. They were each wrapped in their own thoughts of what to say, wondering how they would react, and how the other would react, when they saw Susan. The wait is over and now, they are waiting in the lobby of the YWCA for her to come down.

When Susan came downstairs, she threw her arms around her mother.

Janet said, "How are you, honey?"

"I'm fine and you?" asked Susan, "and you, Mrs. Smith?"

Both ladies answered at the same time. "Fine."

Turning to Susan, Janet says, "I'm hungry, is there somewhere close, where we can get something to eat?"

"There is a very nice cafeteria around the corner on 4th Street. Would you like to go there?" Susan asked.

"Sounds good to me." replied Mrs. Smith.

"And also to me," Mrs. Brown said.

Susan starts to walk away and says, "Let me sign out and we will be on our way. We have to sign in and out each and every time we leave or return to the building. I think it's a bother, but I feel secure because I know that no one is going to be in the rooms unless they belong there."

The three are walking towards the cafeteria when Mrs. Brown says, "I'm so glad they take good care of you. It helps to know you are in a safe place."

"Here we are." Susan exclaims, "The name of the cafeteria is Blue Boar and the food is very good. The other girls and I eat here a lot."

"Let's try to get a table away from the other patrons." Mrs. Brown says, "Kitty and I have some things to discuss with you."

Susan is wondering, *What do they want to talk about? I know Melanie well enough and I know she wouldn't discuss my letter with anyone. Not even James.* She says, "Okay Mom." She gives her mother a smile.

They are seated at a corner table and Mrs. Smith tells them, "I have never seen anyone carry trays like that. Have you?"

"No, I haven't, answered Mrs. Brown.

Susan tells them. "I think it's unique the way they carry the trays on the palm of their hands. They balance two trays at a time, even going up and down the steps. I don't watch them anymore because I know they're not going to drop them."

Mrs. Brown clears her throat and said, "Susan, the reason for our visit... is, well, last week Kitty got a phone call from James. Seems Melanie received a letter from you telling her..." She clears her voice before continuing, "You and James are going to be parents. I want to know if this is true."

Susan blushes, lower her eyes, and says, "Yes, mom, it is true. I am about two and a half months pregnant. This was just something that happened without any plans. James sees me before he sees Melanie, and we have been intimate several times. I certainly didn't want to cause Melanie or James any problems, but now a baby is due. I think James should marry me and take care of our baby."

Mrs. Smith almost choked on her food before saying, "Susan, I'm going to insist on you going to the doctor. I want to make sure you get the best of care. After all, this is my grandchild."

Susan, taken aback thought, *yes, I'll let them take me to the doctor. They won't go into the examination room with me. After James and I are married, I'll have a miscarriage and none will be the wiser.* She says, "I would love for you and mother to take me to a doctor."

"I'm glad that's settled." Mrs. Brown tells her, "We'll call for a doctor in the morning."

CHAPTER 38

The doctor's office was furnished with chairs of leather, several end tables, with a large coffee table in front of a leather couch. The carpet looked several years old, as did the wallpaper. There were several outdated magazines on the tables.

Susan signed in and was thinking, *It won't be long before James and I will be married. We'll have several children. We'll build our house between his parents and my parents. Then, when dad and Mr. Smith get too old to farm, James will tend to both places. Of course, there will be lots of farmhands to help.*

The nurse came to the door and called, "Miss Brown, the doctor will see you now."

All three ladies started for the exam room. The nurse said, "I'm sure there has been a misunderstanding. Miss Brown was the one I called."

Mrs. Brown said, "You are the one who doesn't understand. I am Susan's mother and Mrs. Smith is a very good friend. We will accompany Susan to the exam room and stay with her."

Both Susan and the nurse were startled but the nurse very calmly states, "Very well. Follow me."

The doctor entered the room, took one look at the three women and said, "Hello, ladies, and how may I help you?" Mrs. Brown replied, "My daughter thinks she is pregnant, and Mrs. Smith is the mother of the young man involved. Please examine my daughter and tell us if she is or not. Oh, by the way, we want to be here when you examine her, if you don't mind."

"That'll be fine."

"Mrs. Brown and Mrs. Smith," the doctor said, looking from one to the other, "Susan is not pregnant. In fact, she is still a virgin, so there is no chance of her being pregnant. Now, would either of you like to tell me what is going on?"

Mrs. Smith said, "I'll tell you, doctor. My son is engaged to a lovely young lady, and they are to be married soon. Susan grew up with both my son and his fiancée. She decided James should marry her. She told Melanie she was pregnant with my son's child. Believe me, doctor, Susan will have a comeuppance."

I will have to discuss this with my husband, but Susan will be punished." declared Mrs. Brown.

CHAPTER 39

Leaving the doctor's office, Mrs. Smith says, "I've got to call James. Shall we get a cup of coffee and I can use a pay phone?"

"Absolutely not!" Mrs. Brown answers, "We can after we drop Susan back at the YWCA. This is part of her punishment. I'm not ready to even talk to her."

"Mother, I'm so sorry." Cried Susan, "I love James so much, and I know I can make him happier than Melanie can."

Mrs. Brown ignores Susan and says to Mrs. Smith, "We'll get the coffee in a few minutes." Reconsidering the silent treatment, she turns to Susan, takes her in her arms, and says, "I do love you, but right now, I'm so discussed with you. If I talk to you, I'll say the wrong thing and make matters worse. Also, if you loved James, you'd want him to be happy, not tied to someone he doesn't love."

Susan crying runs into the YWCA and up the stairs without saying goodbye to either lady.

***

"The coffee was what I needed to settle down." Mrs. Brown confided.

Mrs. Smith agreed, "I think we both did. I'll go call James. I saw a pay phone by the door. Be back in a minute."

When James answered the phone, Mrs. Smith blurted the news. "James, I have great news. Susan is not pregnant."

"Hallelujah!" yelled James.

Mrs. Smith said, "I swear, James, the people here in Louisville could hear you."

"Momma, this is the best news I have had in years. I can't wait to tell Melanie, so I'll hang up now. I love you. Bye."

"Bye, son, I love you too."

***

James called Melanie immediately.

Melanie answered the phone, "Hello"

Without introducing himself or saying hello, James says, "Hi, hon, I have some great news. Susan isn't pregnant. We can continue our wedding plans. How is the dress coming? Did you tell your mother or anyone else?"

Laughing Melanie tells him, "That is great news and yes, I did tell John and mom. They will be so happy. I can't wait to tell them. James, we must confront Susan together on your next leave. If we don't, she'll continue to try to break us up."

Scratching his head, James says, "You are right, and as much as I don't want to see her, we'll have to either go to her or have her join us. Until later, my darling. I love you."

"I love you too. Bye." Melanie hangs up the phone and goes in search of John.

John looked up in surprise to see Melanie entering the barn. "This isn't the mess hall, little lady."

Melanie tells him, "No, it isn't, and I didn't think to bring you coffee. I do have some great news. Susan isn't pregnant.

"Now we have another problem. We will have to confront her, and I'm not sure I can be objective, when I talk to her. Right now I would like to scratch her eyes out, maybe hang her from the highest tree and throw poison darts at her."

John couldn't restrain his laughter. "Now, now, you don't want to do anything so drastic. Those acts just might postpone your wedding, because you would be in the pokey. Let's think of something else. I think the best punishment would be to have her give the bridal shower and to have her as one of the bridesmaids."

"Oh come on." Melanie protested, "A bridesmaid? Never! Never! Never! In a million years."

"Think about it." Retorted John, "This would show Susan you forgive her and at the same time she would be punished severely. You would have her where you could keep an eye on her movements."

"Okay, John," Melanie says, "I'll think about it, but I won't promise anything until I have talked to James. I need to get back to start supper, and you need to get back to work. I'll see you at supper."

CHAPTER 40

James made up his mind to confront Susan. *Yes, I'll tell Melanie to pick me up later. I'll call Susan and tell her I want to meet for coffee. I know Susan will meet me because in her mind, I have decided she is the girl for me. I don't think she is a nice person.*

***

Susan had hung up the phone and was dancing around the room. *I think I'll wear the outfit I wore the first time I came to Louisville. I know James realizes how much I love him and we can start planning our wedding. Melanie was never good enough for him. She isn't and wasn't our kind of folks. She would never fit in. I can't wait to see James. I'm sure glad he called me.*

***

James saw Susan as the bus pulled into the station in Louisville. *How could anyone as pretty as Susan be so mean, conniving, and vicious? Well, she is and I'm going to be very stern with her.*

Susan saw James get off the bus and ran to him, "Oh, James, I could hardly wait for this weekend. I know we'll have a good time and I'll make you forget you ever knew Melanie. I'm so glad you didn't make the mistake of marrying her. She isn't our kind of people."

James trying to control his temper said, "And what kind of people is that, the kind that will lie, cheat, connive, and tell vicious lies to get their way? Well, let me tell you right now. If Melanie and I did break up, you'd be the last person I'd come to for comfort. In fact I hope after today, I never see you again."

Susan stepped back. She was so stunned. It took a few moments before she could answer, "Surely, James, you don't mean that. We've been friends since we were infants. My mother and dad are friends with your mother and dad. What would I tell my parents? How would your parents react? You're just angry, but in time, you'll see the humor and then we can start seeing each other."

Clenching his fist and trying not to hit something, James says, "Susan, I always thought you were a nice, intelligent person, who always made the best of any situation. Boy was I wrong! Instead of intelligent, you are conniving. You're only nice when it serves your purpose, and you will do anything to get what you want and I do mean anything. Well, that doesn't work for me. You had better try to meet someone who doesn't know you. They wouldn't believe what I know you are." James turned and walked away. He thought, *I sure hope I calm down before I see Melanie. Maybe a cup of coffee will help.*

CHAPTER 41

When Janet told him about Susan's latest trick, Sam Brown became furious. He said, "Janet we are going to Louisville, NOW! We'll not invite Tom and Kitty because this is between YOUR daughter and us."

Janet had never seen Sam so angry and told him, "Okay, Sam, but I think you should calm down a little before we go."

He stomped his foot and said, "I don't want to calm down. I want to tell YOUR daughter how disappointed, I am, in her."

Janet wrung her hands and prayed, *Please, God, help me to say the right thing to help my husband and my daughter.* Turning to Sam she says, "All right, but let's eat something first."

Sam glares at his wife but concedes, "If you insist."

"I do." Janet tells him. Nothing she said or did helped Sam calm down.

***

Susan was in her room, lying on the bed, crying and thinking, *I wish mom was here. She'd know what to do and how to make things better.*

Just then the call came. "Susan, your mother and dad are here to see you."

"I'll be right down." She answered. Looking into the mirror, she decided to wash her face and put on her makeup.

As Susan descended the stairs, she saw her father pacing back and forth and running his hand through his hair. Susan thought, *mom must have told dad what I did. That's okay. I've always been able to get dad to forgive me. He always lets me do what I want. I can't stay here without seeing James. Dad will let me come back home.*

Sam saw Susan and said, "Hello, Susan. I came up as soon as I heard what you tried to pull on James and Melanie. I am very disappointed in you. I have always thought you as being a considerate, loving, and gracious young lady. I was wrong. You are a conniving, vindictive, malicious, and hateful spoiled brat. Now for your punishment, you will remain here in Louisville, go to school, get good grades, and get a job. Also, you will continue to volunteer at the church. I pray that you will meet a nice young man and fall in love. Don't tell me you loved James, because if you did you'd want him to be happy. No, Susan, you just wanted the prestige of being his wife. Now go upstairs and get your purse. We are going to take you to see Melanie and her parents, so you can apologize.

With horror in her voice, Susan begs, "Dad, I can't face them. Please don't make me go."

Sam with forcefulness in his voice says, "You should have thought of that before you wrote to Melanie."

Susan Looks at her mother, and pleading says, "Mom, can you reason with dad?"

Shaking her head, Janet tells her, "Sorry, this is one time your father is 100% correct. Go get your purse. If it is too late to see Melanie at home, we will take you to the dance, but you will apologize today, to both Melanie and her parents."

Susan was thinking as she went upstairs to get her purse. *I really messed up this time.*

CHAPTER 42

James had finished telling Rowdy, Mary, and Melanie about his meeting with Susan when they heard a car in the driveway.

It's kinda early for dad and mom to be coming by before the dance. I wonder who it can be, thought Melanie.

James says, "One thing about it, Susan wouldn't dare show her face, at least I don't think she would." Sam Brown entered the mess hall and announced, "I brought Susan and Mrs. Brown with me. James, before you say anything, let me assure you that you will not have to see Susan again after today. I can only say Susan wasn't raised to be underhanded, and I hope that both you and Melanie will accept my and Mrs. Brown's apology.

James was the first one to speak, "Okay, you may bring Susan in for a few minutes. If she says one thing out of line, you are to leave immediately. Understood?"

"Yes, James, and I would feel the same way." Mr. Brown states. He goes to the door and motions for Mrs. Brown and Susan to come in.

Melanie's heart went out to Susan. Melanie took one look at her and thought, *Susan has been crying. John is right. I need to extend a hand of friendship to her, but not until I talk to James.*

Susan said, "Melanie, I owe you and James an apology. I am so sorry that I caused you so many problems. Please forgive me."

"Susan," Melanie says, "I understand you are sorry, but I will have to think about forgiving you. Maybe later, I know James has already told you how he feels."

With a catch in her voice, Susan says, "I'll be staying in Louisville, so please, Melanie, if you can forgive me, let me know."

Sam says, "Melanie, how do I find your parents? Susan wants to apologize to them."

"Mr. Brown, you take the road you came here on, go past the horse barns and they live in the last house on the right. You've gone too far if you come to the cornfield."

Taking Susan by the arm, Mr. Brown started toward the door and says, "Let's go, Susan. I want to get started home. Again, let me tell you how sorry I am, James. If you ever need anything, please feel free to call me.

***

Mr. and Mrs. Cox were just getting into their car when the Browns drove into their driveway.

Getting out of the car, Sam extends his hand to Buddy and said, "Buddy, you may or may not be aware of what Susan has tried to do, but I'm here on an errand of good will. Please accept my apology for all the troubles Susan has caused Melanie and James."

With a blank look on his face, Buddy says, "I'm sorry, Sam, but I haven't a clue as to what you are talking about."

Susan interrupts, "I'm sorry, Mr. Cox, but I wrote a letter telling Melanie I was pregnant and James was the father. I tried to apologize to James. He doesn't want to see me ever again. I have apologized to Melanie and she promised to let me know, if she can forgive me. Please, Mr. Cox, accept my sincere apology."

Mrs. Cox was very sympathetic towards Susan. "I think I understand why you did this. But, Susan, God knows what is best for us. Sometimes we don't agree with God, but you'll see. Somewhere down the road you'll meet someone who will sweep you off your feet. Then you'll wonder what you ever saw in James."

"But I love James so much." Susan protested.

"Susan," Mr. Brown says in a stern voice, "I told you earlier, and I'm telling you again; if you really love James you would not have pulled this. You would have rejoiced in his happiness. The next time we come up, we'll bring the Smiths and you will apologize to them also."

"But, dad, Mr. Smith wants to break them up as much as I do."

Mr. Brown asks, "Did Tom smith put you up to this?"

"No, but I'm sure if my plan had worked, Mr. Smith would have jumped for joy."

Mr. Cox replied, "That may have been true at one time. Mr. Smith now knows how deeply James and Melanie love each other. I know this because he told me.

"Well, my darling daughter, it looks as though you have lost completely."

"Buddy, would you and Jane like to go to supper and maybe a movie with us tonight? Sorry Susan, this is part of your punishment. You aren't invited!"

Buddy said, "I'd like to go, how about you Jane?"

She answered. Yes, I would. It sounds like fun."

Mr. Brown extends his hand to Buddy and says, "Okay, we'll meet you in the lobby of the Brown Hotel at 7:00 p.m. Okay?

Buddy says, as he shakes Mr. Brown's hand, "Jane and I appreciate your coming to apologize, but like Melanie, we will have to think about forgiving Susan. We'll see you at 7:00."

CHAPTER 43

The dance wasn't much fun for anyone this night. All thoughts centered on the events of the past week. Melanie, sitting in a chair, twisting her hair and thinking, *Susan is truly sorry. She has been crying and I think she just realized her little caper has cost her James' friendship. I need to talk to someone. Mom and James are too close to the forest to see the trees. I know where John stands, but I need a woman's view. Maybe Mary and her Aunt Grace will help me decide what to do.*

***

Rowdy and Mary talked about the apology, Rowdy said, "I think Susan is truly sorry and won't try anything else. Don't you?"

Mary answered, "Well she has been crying. However, Susan is so selfish. I think she was crying, because James told her he never wanted to see her or hear from her again."

Putting his arm around Mary, Rowdy says, "You could be right. James and Melanie will both want to talk separately to us. We need to really think about what we're going to say."

Standing and taking Rowdy's hand, Mary tells him, "I know and I am going to pray about it. Let's dance and forget their problems."

CHAPTER 44

Sitting at the kitchen table and having his second cup of coffee, Tom is watching Kitty mixing the cake batter for dessert. The phone rings, Kitty says, "Tom, would you mind getting the phone?"

"Okay, honey." He says, "Hello."

"Oh, hi, Sam. How are you?

"2:00 tomorrow, Sure, We'll see you then. Bye."

Hanging up the phone, Tom turns to Kitty and says, "Kitty, do you know why Sam wants us to come over? He's never called before, so why now?"

Kitty answers, "Yes I know and you had better sit down." When Tom is sitting, Kitty with a sigh says, "Susan wrote a letter to Melanie telling her that she was pregnant and James was the father. Jane and I took her to the doctor, and of course she isn't pregnant. We agreed not to tell you or Sam, but I guess Sam found out. We'll know soon enough."

Shaking his head, Tom says, "And this is our son. Poor Melanie."

Walking over to Tom, Kitty puts a comforting hand on his shoulder and says, "Now, Tom, James said he had never been intimate with Susan, and I believe him."

Tom mutters, "We'll see."

CHAPTER 45

James, Rowdy, Mary, and Melanie were sitting in the mess hall, discussing Susan, when John walks in.

He greets them, "Hi, James. Hello, Rowdy, Girls, looks like you all are being very serious.'

Rowdy speaks up, "Yes, we are. Susan wants James and Melanie to forgive her. We were discussing the pros and cons. I'm not sure James could ever trust her not to cause trouble."

John says, "I told Melanie to include Susan in the wedding. Then you can keep an eye on her. Susan is vindictive and will try to cause further trouble. The decision is up to you and Melanie."

James looks at John, "You know, John, you're right. Keep the enemy close at hand, so you know what he's, in this case she, is up to."

Rowdy speaks, "I don't think, if I was you, James, that I could enjoy my wedding, if she was there."

James looking at the group says, "At this point, I'm not sure how I feel. I just want to marry Melanie as soon as possible."

John replied, "That's the best news I've heard today. Set the date and then you will have a united front."

Melanie, twisting her hair, says, "I still have the contract to fill as cook."

"No, Melanie," says Mary, "I can finish out your contract for you. Now before anyone says anything, I just want you to know that I have a selfish motive. Fulfilling your contract would allow me to keep an eye on Rowdy." She lowers her eyes and takes Rowdy's hand.

"Okay." Melanie answers, James and I will decide on a date and let you know when and where."

James says, "Okay, guys, Melanie and I have a lot of things to discuss, so we are going for a walk and will be back later."

"Okay." They all say in unison.

***

Melanie and James walk over to the horse barn and sit down on a small bench.

James takes Melanie's hand, kisses it, and says, "Honey, I will be leaving Ft. Knox in about three weeks. I will have a 30 day leave, and then only God knows where I will be sent. I really want you to go with me as my wife. I know this is short notice, but if we go to war, I may never see you again."

Running her hand along James' cheek, she says, "It is a short time, but I think with mom's and Mary's help, it can be done."

"Good. Shall we be married on the base by a chaplain? Maybe a church in Louisville, or Lexington? How about Tennessee?"

"Oh, James, let's be married here. I'm sure the Van Winkles won't mind. Then every one of the men can attend. We could make it Saturday after next; say about 2:00 p.m., okay?"

"That sounds great."

"That would be perfect. Let's go tell mom and dad. Mom is making my dress, you know. We'll talk about Susan later, but I think John is right, about including her so we can keep an eye on her."

Taking Melanie in his arms, James tells her, "I'll think about it and let you know."

CHAPTER 46

Mr. and Mrs. Cox are getting out of their car as James and Melanie approach them.

Melanie is excited and doesn't greet them but says, "Mom, Dad, James and I decided to marry a week from Saturday. Can you have my dress and Mary's dress finished by then?"

Smiling, Mrs. Cox says, "Of course. Your dress will need to be tried on and then the finishing touches. Where will you be married?"

"I'm hoping the Van Winkles will let me be married here, on the grounds." She answered.

Now excited, Mrs. Cox tells her, "Melanie, did you know the farm has a small chapel?"

"No, I didn't, but that would be perfect."

Before another word could be said, Mr. Cox takes James by the arm and says, "James, we are as useful as a needle in a haystack. Why don't we go outside to talk? Then these two women can gossip and plan on how to make our lives miserable."

Sticking her tongue out at Mr. Cox, Mrs. Cox says, "Oh, come on, Buddy, you know as well as I do; you've loved every minute of our marriage."

Mr. Cox winks at her and says, "You caught me in another lie."

The two men walk away.

As soon as the men left the room, Melanie says, "Mom, John thinks I should involve Susan in the wedding plans. I have very mixed feelings."

Mrs. Cox takes the wedding dress out of the box and says, "Let's try the dress on. Yes, Susan did a very unladylike thing. You do need to forgive her. After all, you and James will be married a very long time. You'll be going from one army base to another for several years. Susan will stay in Louisville. So, involving Susan is like John said: a security measure. James has about three more weeks before his 30 day leave, right?"

"Right, so what can she do? Mary is my maid of honor and I won't have any other attendants." Melanie tells her.

Mrs. Cox asks, "Could James come up with another nice, good looking single guy."

Melanie twisting her hair, says, "Maybe, but James hasn't given me the okay to invite her yet."

With a smile, Mrs. Cox says, "He will. I know because your dad is talking to him now. I don't think I have to do another thing to your dress."

***

When James and Mr. Cox are alone, Mr. Cox says, "Well James, I hate to lose my little girl, but I'm glad it is you, who is stealing her away."

"Mr. Cox, I will always love and care for Melanie. I wish I could have kept Susan from hurting her, but what is done, is done."

"Don't look back but look forward, Susan made her last desperate attempt." Mr. Cox answers, I don't think she will try anything else. Just to be sure I think I would involve her in the wedding, so I could keep an eye on her."

"You know, you're the third person to tell me this." James replies, "I'll discuss it with Melanie."

"Good, you won't regret it one bit." Mr. Cox says, "I'm taking Jane to Louisville tonight. We are meeting the Browns for supper and a movie."

"That's great," James tells him, "maybe Melanie and I should be getting back."

CHAPTER 47

Walking back to the mess hall, Melanie says, "Let's go to the dance with Rowdy and Mary, James. Maybe we'll see the friend of Rowdy's. You know the one who liked Susan. We could ask him to be her escort to the wedding."

Stopping, and staring at Melanie, James exclaims, "Wait just one minute, honey. I haven't said I'll allow Susan to attend the wedding yet."

Melanie puts her hands on her hips and says, "But you will. I know that. After you think about it, you'll forgive her."

James puts his arm around Melanie and starts walking again. "Just Maybe."

***

Mr. and Mrs. Van Winkle were leaving the mess hall, as James and Melanie were approaching. Melanie spoke first, "Good evening, Mr. and Mrs. Van Winkle. It is nice to see you. Please meet my fiancé, James Smith. James, please meet Mr. and Mrs. Van Winkle. We were going to stop by the main house in the morning to speak to you."

Mr. Van Winkle replied, "That is why we're here. Your mother called us and we came over right away."

Mrs. Van Winkle speaks, "Melanie, Mr. Van Winkle and I want to give the barbeque for your reception. Also, we would be honored if you would use our chapel for your wedding. If there is anything else we can do, don't hesitate to ask. I would feel honored if you would include me in the wedding plans."

Melanie with tears of gratitude in her eyes says, "Oh, Mrs. Van Winkle, I'm so overwhelmed. I don't know what to say, Thank you."

James shook hands with Mr. Van Winkle and said, "I will never forget you and thanks so much. Mom and dad will be getting in touch with you, if that's okay."

Mr. Van Winkles says, "By all means. We look forward to meeting them."

CHAPTER 48

Jeff Spencer arrived early to the dance so he could greet Susan as she walked through the door. *They should be arriving at any time. I've looked forward all week for tonight. Susan is so pretty and very nice.* He thought.

The disappointment showed on Jeff's face as Melanie, Mary, James, and Rowdy walked through the door. He wasted no time in walking over to the group and saying, "Hello, how are you all, and where is Susan?"

James and Rowdy exchanged glances and James answered, "Susan couldn't make it tonight. Her parents are in town and they wanted Susan to themselves. I have some great news and maybe, you'd like to be part of it."

"I might, especially if Susan is part of the news." Jeff answered.

James reaches for Melanie and pulling her close, he says, Melanie and I are getting married a week from Saturday at Dream On. Would you consider being Susan's escort? She just moved to Louisville and doesn't know anyone here or in Louisville."

A big grin spread on Jeff's face from ear to ear, as he asks, "Do you want me to wear a tux, suit, or just a nice outfit?"

Laughing, James asks, "I take it the answer is maybe?"

"Okay, James, have your little joke." Jeff answers, "You see that Susan is here next Saturday."

Melanie speaks up, "Now that that is settled, all we have left to plan is the license, chaplain, and Susan.

CHAPTER 49

"Tom," Kitty says, "I just got a phone call from James. The wedding is planned for a week from this Saturday at Dream On. I think we should go to Louisville as soon as possible. Mrs. Cox is making my dress and I feel I should be there to help with the wedding. Don't you?"

"Sure, by all means." Tom answers, "I'll get Sam to look after things here for the next two weeks. You know, since I've gotten to know Melanie and her parents better, I know James made the right choice. I didn't realize how conniving Susan is. She would never have had James' best interest at heart."

Walking over to Tom, Kitty puts her hand on his shoulder and says, "Be sure to tell Melanie that you welcome her to the family."

Patting Kitty's hand, Tom answers, "I will. I do want Sam and Janet at the wedding. It'll be up to James and Melanie whether Susan is invited or not."

***

The Van Winkles are so excited about having the wedding and reception at Dream On. Tim Van Winkle asks Darcy, "Honey, do you remember when we got married?"

"I sure do." Darcy Van Winkle answered, "Do you think we could duplicate some of the same things for Melanie and James?"

Tim asks, "Why don't you go talk to Mrs. Cox and Melanie tomorrow. Let them know we want to be part of the wedding and part of their lives."

CHAPTER 50

Susan is asleep when the phone rings. *Now who would be calling me? Mom and dad left for home. James and Melanie don't want me for a friend, and no one else knows my phone number, much less me.* She thought.

"Hello"

"Hello, Susan, this is Melanie."

"Look, I have been punished enough for what I did. I am sorry and I hope you and James can forgive me someday. However, I am not in the mood to be told off again."

"Quit feeling sorry for yourself. You just made us set the wedding date. I want you to help me with the wedding and come as a guest. Before you say no, listen and then decide. Do you remember Jeff Spencer? He was the tall blond haired guy who danced every dance with you a couple weeks ago?"

Yes." Susan answers, I really wanted to run my hands through his hair. He is so nice but his hair belongs to a girl, so wavy and those grey eyes sparkle every time he laughs."

"Jeff asked for you at the dance Saturday night. He made us promise to ask if he could call you sometime. Susan, Jeff is very nice, and I bet he'd be your escort to the wedding, if you asked him."

"Did you tell him what I did?"

"No, we thought it would be best if you told him, only if you want to."

Susan thought, *I wonder if she knows how this will hurt to see her marry James. Jeff might be a temporary solution to my being lonely.* She said, "Okay, give Jeff my phone number and yes, I'll help you. Is Mary going to help?"

"Mary is my maid of honor and Rowdy will be the best man. We are getting married a week from Saturday at Dream On. I'm glad you will be there, Susan. Maybe, now, we can be friends."

"I'm looking forward to hearing from Jeff. He might take me out sometime."

"I know he will. He was quite taken by you. Call me after you hear from him and let me know when we can get together."

"Okay, I will. Bye"

"Bye."

CHAPTER 51

Tom and Kitty Smith are almost to Louisville, when Tom says, "As soon as I can, I'm going to take Melanie aside and apologize for being so unfair. It'll just be Melanie and me."

"I don't think so," replied Kitty. "You just might say something that would upset her. I think you should apologize in front of her parents and me. Then if you say something that upsets her, we can smooth it over."

Tom sighs, "We'll see. We're not there yet. Do you think we should see Susan?"

Kitty answers, "Maybe, after we see Melanie. Let's find out if Susan is invited to the wedding."

"Kitty, if James is anything like me. Susan won't be invited. James won't talk to her ever again."

"James is a lot like my father, and dad always forgave everyone. I think James will forgive, maybe not forget. I do know Melanie will feel sorry for her, and James will watch her more closely, so she can't cause more trouble."

CHAPTER 52

Mrs. Van Winkle was with Mrs. Cox and Melanie, when Tom and Kitty knocked on the door. Melanie opens the door and Kitty gives her a hug. Melanie then turns to Mrs. Van Winkle and says, "Mr. and Mrs. Smith, this is Mrs. Van Winkle. She and her husband own Dream On. Mrs. Van Winkle, this is Kitty and Tom Smith, James' mother and father."

Mrs. Smith says, "Sorry to come unannounced, but I do want Jane to make my dress."

"Do you have a pattern or something in mind?" Mrs. Van Winkle Asks.

Jane answers, "I promised Kitty, I'd design and make her dress for the wedding."

"Don't forget, you said you'd make the dresses for the bridesmaids." Kitty reminds Jane.

Melanie speaks up, "Mom, why don't we show them my dress. I do need to try it on again."

In unison, Mrs. Van Winkle and Kitty says, "Please do."

Mrs. Cox tells her, "Go put your dress on and come back."

Kitty looks at first one then the other and says, "Tom and I want to be part of the planning. We do want to share in the cost."

Mrs. Van Winkle replies, "We all appreciate your offer, but Mr. Van Winkle and I do not have any children. Melanie is about the age our daughter would have been, had she lived. Please, make us happy by letting us provide the reception. Don't worry, Mrs. Smith, we'll think of something you can spend money on."

Everyone laughed, and Kitty looked at Tom and said, "We've been so concerned about the wedding and reception that we've forgotten about an apartment or a honeymoon."

Tom, with an impish grin, says, "I just thought we'd go on a second honeymoon and let the kids have the house."

Kitty gives Tom a playful slap and answers, "You wouldn't dare. I am surprised that you didn't want to go on their honeymoon."

Tom answers, "I thought of it but didn't think you'd go for it."

Mrs. Van Winkle says, "We could all go on the honeymoon with them. Of course, they may not be speaking to us after we shivaree them."

"This sounds interesting." Tom states, "What do you have planned?"

Mrs. Wan Winkle answers, "Can't tell you now, but will before the wedding. Isn't this fun?"

Before anyone can answer, Melanie enters the room. She walks to the middle as if she is listening to the bridal march and slowly turns around so everyone can get a good look at the dress.

"Oh, my, how beautiful you are." Tom says.

"Both she and the dress are beautiful. Mrs. Van Winkle agrees, "Jane, you've got to make my dress as well. I'll get Lucy to do the cooking, so you will have plenty of time to make all the dresses and the plans for the wedding."

"Thank you, Mrs. Van Winkle. Jane says, "I do want to make the wedding cake."

"By all means; Mrs. Van Winkle states, "Why don't you and Buddy visit with Mr. and Mrs. Smith tonight? Lucy can finish cooking supper."

With gratitude, Mrs. Cox says, "Thank you so much. Melanie, you've had the dress on too long and it's time you went back to your kitchen."

Melanie turns to leave the room and with a wave of her hand says, "Bye everyone, I'll see you later."

CHAPTER 53

Susan couldn't wait to tell Melanie about the phone call from Jeff Spencer.

It's such a good feeling to have someone to talk to, thought Susan. *Jeff sounds like a very nice person. I really enjoyed talking to him. If I enjoy his company Saturday, I'll ask him to escort me to James' wedding. I wish James was marrying me, but I know that will never happen. Maybe Jeff is the guy, maybe.*

***

As soon as Melanie answers the phone, Susan starts talking."Jeff called me this afternoon. Melanie, we talked almost an hour. He is going to pick me up for the dance Saturday night. I promise no trouble if you let me stay with you. I've learned my lesson. You and James will not have any trouble from me. I'm so lucky to have your forgiveness. Please let me stay. Then you and James can get to know Jeff."

Melanie couldn't help laughing. "Okay, Susan, but you'd better behave, because you'll be in enemy territory. If you're not good, we'll all gang up on you."

"Melanie, don't worry. I will be good. I know now why James loves you, and I will do anything to be your friend."

"You can start by forgetting the past couple of weeks. We'll never mention it again. Okay?"

"Susan says, "Forgotten. Shall Jeff and I come to your place Saturday or just meet you at the dance?"

Melanie answers, "Meet us at the dance. That will give you more time to get to know him. I'm sure the guys will make sure his intentions are honorable."

"I would hope so; I wouldn't want to go through another pregnancy."

Melanie laughed and says, "See you Saturday at the dance."

"Okay, Bye." Susan hangs up the phone, puts her chin in her hand and thinks, *I hope this works out.*

CHAPTER 54

Capt. Dunn called the bugler in and asked, "Can you play anything else beside 'Reveille' and 'Taps?'"

"Yes sir, you name it and I can play it."

"Good, can you play, 'I Love You Truly?'"

"I've played it at a lot of weddings."

Capt. Dunn states, "As you know, James Smith is getting married Saturday in Lexington, Kentucky. I'd like you to play as they come out of the chapel. Do not mention this, as I want it to be a big surprise."

CHAPTER 55

James is pacing the floor, looking in the mirror and asking for the hundredth time, "Rowdy, you do have the ring? Do I look okay? You don't think Melanie will back out, do you? What time is it? I don't want to be late."

"Will you calm down? Rowdy says, "I hate to see you when the first child is born."

Running his hand through his hair, James answers, "That'll be awhile yet."

"I hope so." Rowdy tells him, "You look nice in your uniform. Do you know where you'll be stationed?"

"No, but I requested Officer's Training School."

Rowdy asks, "Do you know where the schools are located?"

"There are several around the country, so I won't know for a few days, until I get my orders. Melanie and I will have 30 days to move and get settled. Today is the happiest day of my life."

Rising to his feet, Rowdy says, "It's time. Let's go."

***

As Melanie entered the chapel, she thought, *The chapel is so pretty, with the white and blue bows on each of the pews. Mom is so talented, thinking to use the leftover white satin from my wedding gown and the leftover blue satin from Mary's dress. Mom even dried some roses to put in the center of the bow. It was fun decorating the chapel with Mary, Susan, Mrs. Smith, Mrs. Van Winkle, and mom. Susan has a nice sense of humor and I hope it works out with Jeff. He really likes her.*

What a sight greeted everyone as Melanie and James came out of the chapel. James reached over and kissed Melanie as flash bulbs and cameras snapped. A bugler was playing 'I Love You Truly' and soldiers stood on each side of the path, in front of the chapel their wives and girlfriends stood with the group at the end of the line. The workers and their wives and girlfriends were all throwing rice.

Tom Smith turns to Capt. Dunn and says, "Well, Dunn, this was a great idea. I'm glad you thought of it."

Shaking his head, Capt. Dunn tells him, "Sorry, Tom, I didn't think of it. I received a phone call from Mr. Van Winkle, and I couldn't turn him down."

"The Van Winkles have given Melanie a great wedding and reception."

Capt. Dunn agrees, "Yes, they have. By the way, Tom, Mr. Van Winkle wants you, Buddy Cox, and me to join him at the cottage. You know the one the kids will occupy until James' 30 days is up."

"Okay, Dunn, I'll tell Buddy." And Tom starts to walk away.

James sees his father and calls, "Dad, would you bless the food?"

Walking to the head of the table, Mr. Smith says, "Sure, son."

James taps a spoon against the edge of a glass and announces, "Could we have your attention, please? My father, Tom Smith, is going to bless the food. Then you all can line up to eat."

Bowing his head and folding his hands, Mr. Smith prays, "Dear God, thank you for this food we are about to receive from your bounty. May it nourish our body and our soul, in the name of Jesus. Amen."

James calls out, "Let's eat."

Melanie whispers to James, "Everything is so good and I think everyone is having a good time, but as soon as we cut the cake, let's slip off. Okay?"

James asks, "Do we have to wait that long?"

"Yes," Melanie answers, "We owe it to everyone who came."

With a frown on his face, James reluctantly says, "Only, if you say so."

***

Mr. Van Winkle comes up to Tom and says, "Okay, Tom, slip out with Buddy and Capt. Dunn to the cottage. We'll make this a night, they'll never forget. See you in a few minutes at the cottage."

Tom managed to tell each of the men and they had slipped away without anyone noticing. At the cottage, Mr. Van Winkle tells them, "Okay, guys, we are going to shivaree James and Melanie. First we take just enough slats out of the bed, so it will fall when they lay down. While the slats are exposed, we will connect this bell underneath so it will ring, when they sit down. Next, we put the sheet across the bed, instead of long ways. It makes a ridge at the top and the bottom of the bed. Now, we rig the camera to catch the expression on their faces, when they come in the door. Let's get to work. I figure we have less than a half an hour.

"When we get back, we must watch Melanie and James real close. When they leave, we'll give them a half an hour. Then, we'll get most of the crowd to go with us. We'll have all kinds of noise makers to get them up."

Tom said, "This sounds like a lot of trouble for nothing."

"Come on Tom," Mr. Van Winkle says, "this is a family tradition. It's a lot of fun."

Tom shaking his head and with doubt in his voice says, "I'll take your word for it. What do you want me to do?"

***

Melanie and James cut the cake, danced with each other, the parents, and opened the dance to everyone. As soon as everyone was dancing, Melanie whispered to James, "Let's leave."

Without answering, James dances Melanie to the edge of the dancers and pretending to go to the punch bowl, they slip out of sight.

CHAPTER 56

James insisted on carrying Melanie across the threshold and almost dropped her when the flash on the camera went off.

"What was that?" Melanie inquired.

James answers, "I don't know, but I'll turn the light on and see if I can find out."

"James, I think our parents have rigged the bed to shivaree us. It makes good memories. So be a good sport, and let's pretend nothing happened."

He looks lovingly at his bride and says, "Whatever you say, my love. Fifty years from now, I'll tell you what I'm really thinking about all this."

Melanie thinks a minute and says, "Honey, we only have a short time, so, let's get busy. Help me with the bed."

"What!" James answers in shock.

"Please, James, just do as I ask."

James is perplexed, "Okay, what about the bed?"

"Let's pull the covers off neatly; we can put them back, without a lot of trouble. If I'm right, the sheet is short changed. That'll mean some of the bed slats are missing. Look under the bed, while I remove the sheet."

James' voice is full of wonder, "You're right. There is also a bell."

"Melanie says, "Okay, be careful and slide the slats out where I can get them. I'll put the slats back while you remove the bell. Then we must leave. They'll be coming any second. We'll go out the back door and hide. Not a word about what we did. Let them wonder."

"Sounds good to me." James says, as they go out the back door.

They found the perfect spot to watch the cottage. Melanie sees the guests coming and says, "Here they come and are they in for a surprise. Don't get noisy; we don't want them to know we're not in the house."

James asks, "How long are we going to stay hidden?"

"Not very long," Melanie answers, "here they come."

Mr. Van Winkle gives the orders, "Let's surround the house. Tom, you take a group around back. Dunn, you go to the east side and Buddy, you take the west side. I'll stay in front. When everyone is in position, about five minutes, start the noise. The noisier the better."

"Let's go."

Melanie couldn't help it. She started laughing, and said, "With all the noise, I don't think they will ever hear us. Let's circle and come in front of the cottage."

"Okay." James says.

Mr. Van Winkle was the first to see Melanie and James. "We've been fooled. They didn't come home, but went walking instead. It's a good thing, the moon was shining."

Melanie says, "I guess you all want to see the inside."

"Of course," Mr. Van Winkle says, "that's what all the noise is for, to keep you up and to celebrate with one last toast to your happiness. There's champagne and glasses in the kitchen. Let's get some lights on and finish up our celebration."

***

Melanie and James noticed the men going into a huddle. Melanie glanced at James and they both almost laughed out loud.

Mr. Van Winkle with wonderment in his voice asked, "Hey Tom, are you sure you fixed that bell to ring, when you set on the bed?"

"Of course I did," He answered, "but the bed didn't fall either. Buddy did you and Dunn take out enough slats?"

Mr. Van Winkle asks, "Do you know what I think?"

In unison the men say, "Tell us."

"Okay." Mr. Van Winkle states, "I think they found out about our tricks. They are enjoying watching us, wondering when the bed will fall."

"Tom scratches his head and says, "Let's confront them before we go home. How about now? Everyone will enjoy the laugh."

Capt. Dunn steps to the middle of the room and loudly announces, "Attention, everyone. Tom smith has something to say."

"This should be an apology, because, Mr. Van Winkle, Capt. Dunn, Mr. Brown, and myself, tried to shivaree Melanie and James. They must have found out and corrected everything. The bell didn't ring, when the bed was set on and it didn't fall."

James says, "Yes, dad, Melanie heard about Mr. Van Winkle's wedding day and figured you'd try the same thing. I wish I had had a camera and taken your picture, when you were in your little huddle."

Everyone breaks out in laughter with the men slapping each other on the back and the women gathering around Melanie. They congratulated her on outsmarting the men.

Mr. Van Winkle looks at everyone, laughs, and says, "On this note, I think we should all leave."

Melanie goes to the door, opens it, and says, "Thanks for coming. This is one day, we'll never forget; at least I won't."

With a chuckle, James added, "I will always wish I'd had a camera to take the picture of the men. Good night to all, drive safely, and come see us before we move."

In unison the crowd tells them, "Good night and good luck to you both."

CHAPTER 57

James takes Melanie in his arms and says, "Honey, I will know in a couple of days where I will be sent. My basic training is almost over. Capt. Dunn suggested that I apply for Officer's Training School."

Melanie kisses James on the cheek and tells him, "I'll start packing tomorrow, so we can move at the same time. You can help me find a place to live."

"Capt. Dunn said they have housing on the bases and he thinks we could qualify for one of the units." James says, "You need to remember, wherever, I'm sent, I want you with me. However, if the situation in Europe gets worse, the United States will have no choice but to go to war. I want you to promise; if I go to war that you will either return here or go stay with my parents."

Clinging tightly to James, Melanie says, "Oh, James, I do promise, but I pray we will never be separated, even for one day. I keep praying that we won't go to war."

"I pray the same thing." James says as he brushes her hair back from her face. "Hitler is determined to rule the world, and we can't let him get away with it."

Taking James' hand and leading him towards the bedroom, Melanie says, "I know, but I'm so tired, let's just go to bed. We'll cross that bridge when we come to it."

CHAPTER 58

Having breakfast and finishing her cup of coffee, Mrs. Van Winkle motions for the server to come to her. "Mayme, please ask Jane Cox to come here, now."

Mayme answers, "Yes, Ma'am." and leaves the breakfast nook to seek Jane.

Jane is busy washing the cooking utensils, when Mayme tells her; she is wanted by Mrs. Van Winkle. Jane thinks, *I wonder what she wants. Well I'll have to go see.*

***

Walking into the breakfast nook, Jane asks, "You wanted to see me?"

"Jane, I want to tell you how pleased we are with your cooking. However, that's not the reason, I asked you to come see me.

"Remember at the wedding, I told you how much I liked Melanie's dress. Well, Mr. Van Winkle and I discussed this and we would like for you to become my official seamstress. Before you say anything, let me continue. You'd do all the designing and sewing of my clothes. We'd want you to design and sew the jockey silks. Also, you would be in charge of any mending and the making of curtains, slip covers and so forth. There would be an increase in your pay, starting today, if you decide to do this.

"As you have seen, Mr. Van Winkle and I are not greedy people, so if someone would want you to make them an outfit and pay you, we'll tell you to do it."

Jane puts her hand to her mouth, straightens her shoulders, and says, "I don't know what to say except, thanks. My dream since I was a child was to be a dressmaker. I had given up on it. There aren't enough words to describe how I feel."

Clearing her throat, Mrs. Van Winkle says, "I have another request. Is there someone on the kitchen staff that could take your place?"

Without hesitation, Jane answers, "I think either Olive or Pansy could take over and please you more than I do."

"Good, Jane, would you send both ladies to me?"

"Yes Ma'am."

"Please call me Darcy."

"Thanks again, Darcy." Jane says as she leaves the breakfast nook.

CHAPTER 59

Capt. Dunn, sitting at his desk holding the orders for James Smith, thought, *I'm glad James made Officer's Training School. I know he will make a good officer. I hope he'll make the army his career. Melanie has moved around most of her life, so she may enjoy army life.*

James comes into the office to pick up his orders and Capt. Dunn greets him, "Hello, James. Here are your orders. You will be transferring to Ft. Benning, Georgia for Officer's training. You have a 30 day leave beginning tomorrow at twelve hundred hours. I have spoken to Lt. Dudley about housing and they do have a vacancy. I took the liberty of securing the house for you."

James puts his orders in his pocket and says, "Thank you so much. Melanie and I will never forget you."

Shaking hands with James, Capt. Dunn tells him, "Just make us all proud of you and good luck."

"Thank you, sir." James says as he salutes, turns and walks out the door.

***

The first thing James does, when reaching the barracks, is phone Melanie. "Honey, I just received my orders and I will be leaving tomorrow. I thought, if it is okay with you, we would spend a couple of days with your parents, leave, and spend a couple of days with my parents. Then we'll go to Ft. Banning, and check out the living arrangements. Okay?"

"That sounds great." Mary tells him, "I'll call Mary as soon as we hang up.

"Honey, I don't want to get too overconfident, but Jeff Spencer has been giving Susan, the 'bum's rush.' She really likes Jeff. I don't think she will be giving us any more trouble."

With a sigh of relief, James says, "Thank God. Anyway, we'll be out of state and away from everyone. Do you think you can stand being alone with me?"

"I might consider doing that." Melanie Laughed.

"I need to hang up as I need to pack and get ready to see my wife." James tells her, "If I have time, I'll stop by to see you."

Laughing, Melanie says, "I love you, until tomorrow. Bye, my love."

"I love you too. Bye sweetheart." James hangs up the phone.

CHAPTER 60

Coming into the kitchen from the mailbox, Jane Cox says, "Look Buddy, we got a letter from Melanie."

"Let's read it now. That is, if supper will wait a little while." Buddy replies.

"I was hoping you'd say that." Jane answers.

> Dear Mom and Dad,
> We did spend a few days with Mr. and Mrs. Smith. I'm sorry to say, Mrs. Smith isn't doing too well. She had another spell while we were there. I have a feeling it won't be long before Mrs. Smith will need 24 hour care.
> Mr. Smith was very nice to me, but I can't help feeling that he would have rather James married someone else. He did tell me he was glad James married me and that he considers me his daughter. He told me, he would always treat me as his daughter. We'll see. I hope he is sincere.
> I've been a little homesick. I miss our talks after work and the advice I always got from you both as well as the hugs.
> Tell Mr. and Mrs. Van Winkle, thanks again for everything, including the '39 Chevy Coupe, they sold James. I know they underpriced the car. Mr. Smith said we got a bargain.
> The Van Winkles have proved to be good Christian people. I will write them in a few minutes.
> James and I did get housing on the base. It has two bedrooms and is the right size for two people. The extra bedroom is for you, the Smiths, and anyone else to visit and have a place to stay. I've met several wives, but Ashley Demons is the one, I'm closest to. Her husband is in James' classes. She took me to the PX, and mom, you

wouldn't believe the prices! It has everything you need or want, at prices way below the stores off base.

Ashley's husband, Darrell, plays the guitar. They sing together and I think they are good. She told me they met at an amateur night, the high school held as a fund raiser.

Darrell won 1st prize and Ashley won 2nd. They talked, decided to sing together, and after a year, discovered they loved each other and got married. The four of us have had a couple of cookouts and of course, we go to church and the movies together.

Speaking of couples, do you hear from Susan? I haven't heard from her and wondered if she is still dating Jeff? How does Mary like cooking for the men? Have Mary and Rowdy set a date yet? I bet if we go to war, Mary and Rowdy would get married immediately.

Have you heard from Mr. and Mrs. Brown? We didn't get a chance to see them while we were in Tennessee.

I did get all the thank-you notes mailed last week. It seems so strange not to have to cook for all those men.

Mom, how is your dressmaking enterprise going? Maybe before long you can quit Mrs. Van Winkle and have your own shop. I think that would be great.

Tell John and everyone we said hello. Maybe we'll get to stop by when James finishes school.

Hope everyone is well. I love you both.

Love,

Melanie and James

As Jane puts the letter back in the envelope, Buddy says, "I wonder if she knows how much we miss her."

"Buddy, we can't get melancholy. Melanie must be encouraged, not made more homesick. Let's eat supper."

"Okay, Jane, but I still miss her."

CHAPTER 61

Susan thought, *I need to write to Melanie, but I really haven't had time. Jeff and I have decided if we still feel the same in six more months, we'll start planning our wedding. I don't know how I could have thought I was in love with James. I'm glad Melanie forgave me. I'm glad James asked Jeff to be my escort to their wedding. Jeff still laughs about that. He said he was trying to figure a way to be invited, because he wanted to be with me. A lot certainly can happen in a few short months.*

Mom and dad will be up this weekend. Jeff has promised to spend a lot of time with them. I know dad will really like Jeff once he gets to know him. His father, Walter Spencer, is a professor at the University of Kentucky. He teaches agriculture and applies what he teaches to his acreage. Their farm is down the road from the Dearing's farm.

***

The phone is ringing and Melanie hurryingly wipes her hands on her apron before answering. "Hello."

"Hi Melanie, I couldn't wait another minute to tell you the good news. I haven't even told mom and dad yet."

"Wait a minute. Who is this? Do you have the correct Melanie?"

"I'm sorry, Melanie. It's just, I'm so excited. This is Susan. You know, the one who caused you so much trouble and now considers you one of her best friends."

Laughing, Melanie says, "Susan, I'm going to make a guess. You got a job or Jeff asked you to marry him, or both!"

"Right on both accounts. I told Jeff I would marry him next year. I want to be sure we have a love like mom and dad's and like yours and James. I want you to be my matron of honor and Mary as one of my bridesmaids. Say you will Melanie, because without you forgiving me and extending your friendship, Jeff and I wouldn't have dated."

"Of course, Susan, I will. I'm sure mom will be willing to help in any way she can. Now tell me about the job."

"I'm working for a father/son law firm. Mr. Adams is very nice and a good teacher on what he wants done. His son is a different item altogether. Ben Adams is not married and thinks he is God's gift to all women. Ben thinks I should be all goo goo about him, because he is good looking, has a good sense of humor, and lots of money. Ben is the most arrogant person, I have ever met. Anyway, after meeting Jeff, who is gentle, fun, and good looking, I could never settle for someone like Ben, regardless of his position in town."

"It sounds like Jeff is the love of your life, if you are comparing every bachelor you meet to him."

"Oh, Melanie, I don't know how I ever thought James should marry me instead of you. Dad was right. I was just thinking of the prestige."

"Susan," Melanie says with an authoritative voice, "that is in the past, and I refuse to speak of it again. Please say you will put it out of your mind also."

"Okay, Melanie, I promise. When I get some time off, Jeff and I plan on visiting you and James, if that is okay."

"By all means, do come. It would be good to see you."

Looking at her watch, Susan says, "It's time for me to go to work. I'll let you know when we are coming."

"Bye."

"Bye."

CHAPTER 62

Melanie rushes into James' arms, as he comes through the door. She kisses him and says, "Honey you'll never guess who called this morning."

Kissing his wife again, James says, "Well, don't keep me waiting. Who was it?"

Melanie pulls away and says, "Susan called to tell me two pieces of news."

"Oh, really, and what has *your* Susan cooked up this time to cause trouble?"

"Now, James, Susan has come to realize you were just a fascination for her. She is no longer interested in you. I know you are disappointed but after you treated her so mean, I don't blame her. Anyway, you are married, and I'm sure Susan's dad and mom would love to see her involved with a married man." Melanie gives a little laugh.

James reaches for her and says, "Come here you little vixen. I want another kiss."

Casting her eyes downward Melanie answers, "Only if you are good."

"I promise I'll listen to what Susan said."

Melanie walks over to James, and says, "Here's your kiss on the cheek."

"OH NO, you don't!" James grabs her and gives her a great big kiss.

Melanie says, "Now be serious and listen. Susan has agreed to marry Jeff Spencer next year. She called to see if I would be her matron of honor. I told her I'd let her know after I talked to you. Oh, she and Jeff want to come for a visit. I told her to let me know when. I think it would be fun. You could room with Jeff and I'd room with Susan."

James looking stern, says, "It looks like you and Susan aren't looking for approval. You just want us poor, defenseless, men to think our opinion matters. Right!"

"Melanie, you can tell Susan you'll be her matron of honor and yes, she and Jeff can come to visit. Jeff needs to be warned about getting married," and under his breath, James added, "especially to Susan."

Melanie starts putting the food on the table and says, "It's time for supper. Since you've been good, I'll feed you."

CHAPTER 63

Mr. Smith goes to his wife's bedroom, opens the door and sees Kitty lying on the floor. "Kitty! Kitty! Please God, let her be okay. Kitty, honey, can you hear me? I've called for an ambulance. Hang on till they get here."

The ambulance arrives and the attendants have checked Mrs. Smith over. Turning to Mr. Smith, one of the attendants says, "We're taking your wife to the hospital. It might be a good idea to call your son. Let them know she has had a very severe spell this time."

"I will later, after I've talked to the doctor. I'll meet you at the hospital."

***

Melanie was very engrossed in her book and didn't hear the phone ringing. Then it dawned on her and she jumped up and ran to the phone. "Hello"

"Hi, Melanie, This is your father-in-law, and I hope you're sitting down."

"What is wrong?" She asked.

"My Kitty is in the hospital. We took her by ambulance last night. I waited to call until I talked to the doctor. The news isn't good.

"Please, Mr. Smith, tell me what the doctor said."

"Kitty, my darling Kitty, is very ill. The doctor says that Kitty's heart is wearing out. He said she will have to rest a lot more than she has been. In fact he told me to look for a live-in maid to take care of her. Melanie, I don't know what I would do without her. I don't know what I'm supposed to do or where to turn. I feel so disorganized. Please help me, Melanie."

"I will call James, immediately, and either he or I will call you back."

"Thank you, Melanie. I knew you and James would help. I'll talk to you later. Bye."

"Bye."

CHAPTER 64

Melanie thought, *Now, what should I do? I don't know how to reach James. Besides, what could we do? James belongs to the army and the officers either grant or deny a leave for any reason. Should I call Capt. Dunn for help and advice or just wait until James gets home?*

The phone broke into her thoughts, but Melanie hesitated before answering. *I don't want to talk to anyone. Oh well, maybe I need some conversation to help me make a decision.*

"Hello."

"Hi, it's Ashley and I wanted to chat for a minute. Several of us are going for coffee this afternoon and thought you might like to join us."

"I'm not sure right now. My father-in-law called. James' mother is in the hospital. She is very ill and will need 24 hour care when she goes home. I feel I need to contact James, but I'm not sure how to go about it."

Ashley says, "Go to coffee with us, and I'm sure some of the ladies will know the answer."

"What time are you going?" Melanie asks.

"We'll meet at my house between 1:00 o'clock and 1:30." Ashley answers.

"Okay, I'll meet you, however, if I can't go, I'll call you."

"Bye until later." Ashley says.

"Bye." Melanie hangs the phone up and thinks, *I think I will call Capt. Dunn. He did tell me that if I needed anything, he would try to help.*

***

Capt. Dunn came walking through the door to his office as the phone rang. He raced the few feet and picked up the receiver. "Capt. Dunn speaking."

"Good morning, Capt. Dunn. This is Melanie Smith, James' wife and Tom Smith's daughter-in-law."

"How nice it is to hear from you, Melanie. What can I do for you?"

"My mother-in-law is seriously ill, and I do not know the protocol to contact James. Do you mind walking me through the steps to take?"

"Of course not," Capt. Dunn says, "first you contact his officer in charge. I'll look up his name and phone number for you. Tell him the problem. The officer will then decide whether James should be told then or wait until he sees you this evening. The army doesn't like to give emergency leave for anything but death. Tom knows this, so don't feel bad if you are told this can wait until James gets home."

"Thank you so much for your help, and since I now know how the army works, I'll just wait until James comes home."

"Good thinking. Tell Tom my thoughts and prayers are with him."

"Thanks again. I won't take up any more of your time. Bye."

"Tell all I said hello. Bye."

CHAPTER 65

James enters the house, sees Melanie, and gives her a hug and a kiss.

Melanie asks, "How were your studies today?"

"Okay, I guess. I couldn't seem to get into the mood to listen. It was as if I was waiting for something to happen, but didn't know what." James answers.

With a sigh and leading James to a chair, Melanie sits on his lap. "Honey, I wanted to call you this morning. I talked to Capt. Dunn and he advised me to wait until you got home to night. He said the army wouldn't do anything unless there was a death and only then if the deceased was a very close relative."

"What is the news?" James asks.

"They took your mother by ambulance to the hospital last night. Your dad called this morning, after he had talked to the doctor. Her heart is wearing out, and she will need 24 hour care when she goes home." Melanie answers.

Stoking Melanie's back and with a faraway look, James says, "I would hate to be separated from you for even a day, but dad needs someone to help him. Mom likes and respects you. I'm an only child, so the burden of helping my parents falls on us. Now, mind you, the decision is yours to make. Have you told your parents?"

"No, honey, I haven't called mom. I called Capt. Dunn because I wasn't sure what the army's protocol was. I told your dad you would call him, when you got home. As much as I want to stay here with you, I think I should leave as soon as possible for your parents' house. That way I can help prepare the house for your mother's home coming."

"Yes, dear," James says, "I agree with you. I'll call dad, after I call the bus station for prices and the schedule."

"Honey, I could drive and it wouldn't take as long."

"No, I won't hear of you driving to Tennessee by yourself. Anyway, I'll need the car to get groceries and to move our things when school is finished."

Twisting her hair, Melanie says, "You're right. I'll take the bus.'

***

Mr. Smith is sitting by the phone, drinking his third cup of coffee, when the phone rings. "Hello."

"Hi, Dad, how's mom?"

"She seems to be holding her own right now. I'm not sure when she will get out of the hospital. The doctor did say she would need 24 hour care."

"Dad, Melanie and I talked it over, and Melanie will leave as soon as possible. She wants to come and prepare the house for mom. She'll stay as long as she is needed."

"I really appreciate that, son, especially since you are still on your honeymoon. Melanie's coming here for an indefinite time will keep you apart. You don't know where you will go after the school ends. They may send you some place where you can't get home but once a year. How would you feel about that?"

"Dad, we may be separated longer and quicker than you think, especially if Hitler keeps trying to rule all the countries in Europe. If we go to war, Melanie couldn't go with me. She would either return to her parents or stay with you until my return. I think God just helped us make the decision about which parents to stay with."

"It seems to me, you and Melanie have discussed the arguments. Your mother will be really pleased. So when will Melanie be here?"

"She is packing now. We will put her on the bus at 7:00 a.m. and she should be in Jackson, Tennessee, by 7:00 p.m. You know the bus stops at every town."

"Son, I'll meet her bus, and I know your mother will be glad."

"Okay, Dad. I need to help Melanie. Tell Mom hello for me, and please keep me informed."

"Sure, son. Bye."
"Bye."

CHAPTER 66

"How was the trip, Melanie?" Mr. Smith asks, as he picks up her luggage.

"Slow, very slow," She answers, "maybe I was overanxious, but the bus stopped at every town and sometimes, it made two or three stops, in the same town. We also, had half an hour stop, so we could get something to eat. How is Mrs. Smith?"

"She is doing better. The doctor said she might come home the first part of next week."

"That's great news. It looks like I got here just in time." Melanie says.

"Yes, you did, Melanie. I want you to know, I'm glad James married you. It seems my son is a better judge of character than I am. It's good that James inherited my hardheadedness. Otherwise, he'd married Susan. I'm afraid Susan wouldn't have come to help us as you have."

"Thank you, Mr. Smith. Let's go home, so I can start preparing for Mrs. Smith."

***

A few days after Mrs. Smith came home from the hospital, she calls Melanie to her side, "Melanie, you have been a Godsend. It is so good of you to come and look after us."

"Mrs. Smith, you don't have to thank me; that is part of being a family."

Mrs. Smith takes Melanie's hand and says, "Mr. Smith and I have been talking. We would like to give you and James the 100 acres, on the corner of our farm. You know, the north side faces Bristow Road and the east side faces Evans Road."

Squeezing Mrs. Smith hand, Melanie exclaims, "Oh, Mrs. Smith, that is way too generous, but I know James will be pleased."

"The other thing we'd like to do is have your house built. You can help plan and decorate it anyway you like. By the time the house is built, I'll be well enough, and you'll only need to stay with me in the daytime."

"James and I always planned to build our home together. I will tell him about your plans and see what he says."

"Okay," Mrs. Smith says, "I'm sure James will tell you to go ahead and plan the house. You see, Melanie, I think James would love the idea of you being in a house of your own."

CHAPTER 67

The phone was ringing as James came through the door. He knew without answering, who it was. Melanie always called just as he got home. After, the greetings and Melanie had told him of his parents' plans to give them the land and to build their house, she waited for his answer.

"Honey, your news is great. It'll be terrific to come to our home. Just think you will have designed and decorated it with love. How could I not like it, Melanie? Any place on earth would be heaven if I was with you, even more so in our own home. And think, dad will continue farming our 90 acres on shares. Honey, have you figured what that'll mean to us?"

"No," Melanie answers, I didn't do the math. Will it be the standard split, 60/40, 60% for him and 40% for us?"

"Honey, the crops will be split 50/50, 50% for each of us.

Melanie asks, "Then you want me to tell them to make the deed to both of us and to start the house?"

"Yes, honey. This is exciting. I love you and I miss you. It won't be long until I get a leave. Then I'll get to spend some time with you."

"I love you too." Melanie says, "As much as I hate to, I'm going to tell you bye, as it's time for your mother's medicine."

"Bye, my love." And James hangs up the phone.

CHAPTER 68

As Melanie put the last dish in the cabinet, she thought, *the house couldn't have been finished at a better time. I'll have our first Thanksgiving dinner in our home. Mr. and Mrs. Van Winkle plus mom and dad will be here. Susan and Jeff are driving down with Mary and Rowdy. Mr. and Mrs. Brown are coming along with Mr. and Mrs. Smith. James got a few days off. I hope everything turns out okay.*

The house is picture perfect. Our home is a beautiful cottage, a door between two windows, in front, with a porch across the front. I'm so glad Mr. Smith let me pick out the trim, a pretty blue and the porch swing is the same color. James will like the layout. You enter the parlor with the dining room just beyond. The door from the dining room leads to the hall with three bedrooms and a bath, plus a door to the basement. The other door in the dining room leads to the kitchen.

I sure hope James likes my decorating. It'll be good to see everyone again. It'll be great to have James hold me.

***

Melanie is trying to get dinner ready and says, "Please, James, I'm trying to get dinner ready. I love you and I'm so glad you are home, even for a little while, but please go sit down; walk over to your dad's, or do something, besides follow me from room to room."

"Honey, why don't you let me help? I do know my way around a kitchen or did you forget I've had KP duty in the army? Besides, I don't want you out of my sight."

With a sigh, Melanie says, "Okay, you win. Start peeling potatoes or you might want to set the table."

"What if I do both?"

"Good, do both." Melanie tells him.

***

The men retired to the parlor, while the women finish cleaning the kitchen. Each man commented on how good the meal was and then they got into a serious discussion on the war situation in Europe.

"James," Sam Brown says, "What have you heard about the war in Europe?"

"Not any more than you. It does seem we are headed to war, if Hitler keeps pushing our allies. I'm not sure I approve of his 'Master Race' theory."

Mr. Van Winkle response, "Nor I, I realize if you take only the strongest, the characteristics you want, like Hitler's blond, blue eyed people, then you have a very strong blond, blue eyed race, but the race is doomed. Somewhere along the way the race would have to inbreed with each other. We know what happens next. The race becomes mentally disabled with all the impurities showing up."

"That's right," Tom Smith joined in. "this is the very reason we try very hard not to inbreed our livestock. When the livestock are inbred, you get uncontrollable animals."

Buddy Cox spoke up, "I can't understand why Hitler has turned against the Jew so much. I understand he's Jewish."

"Yes, he is," Rowdy says, "I think he is trying to rule the world. However, like Napoleon, the countries will band together and not allow it to happen. If it means we will go to war, we will."

Jeff waited a few minutes and said, "I'm ready to fight. I wouldn't want to leave Susan but the fight for freedom is more important to everyone, than my wanting to stay safe and secure with my future wife. You see, if Hitler would conquer all of Europe, he would come after us next. I, for one, would rather fight him on his territory, than on ours."

The men in unison said, "Amen."

CHAPTER 69

James, lying on his bunk and thought, *What a great weekend it was with Melanie and our closest friends. Melanie is so pretty. I'm fortunate to have her. Even dad said I was smarter than he was, because I knew Melanie was the wife I needed. I certainly am glad dad owned up to his mistake. Mom said she wouldn't know what to do without her. What is going on? The bugler is playing 'Reveille' on Sunday morning. Well it means we have to fall in regardless, so much for Sunday.*

***

"Now hear this." The Capt. announces, "All leaves are cancelled as of 30 minutes ago. The Japanese have bombed Pearl Harbor. We were not prepared. President Roosevelt is expected to announce World War II today. A word of advice: start packing, and call home. Sorry, but we don't know where you will be sent or when. Most of you would have been shipping out in a couple of weeks, just sooner than we thought."

***

Tom, Kitty, and Melanie are sitting in the parlor, listening to the radio when the news is announced by President Franklin Roosevelt. He states, "We were bombed by the Japanese this morning. They attacked Pearl Harbor and destroyed a number of our ships. I and my cabinet feel that we haven't a choice but to declare war.

Melanie gave out a cry of distress. Tom and Kitty sat motionlessly, just looking at each other in disbelief.

Melanie spoke first, "Please excuse me. I need to be alone."

Tom says, "By all means, hon. After you've had a good cry, come back over. We'll try to reach James then."

"Thank you." Melanie says, as she goes out the door, to go home.

Tom says, "I never thought I'd see the day, our son would be fighting in a war. It isn't pretty. I was hoping James would be stationed back at Ft. Knox, so he could come home a lot. Now only God can protect him."

"I know, Tom, but at least he knows Melanie will always be cared for."

Tom wasn't paying attention to his wife and says, "At least the worry of Melanie's wee being is off his mind. Honey, I need to call Buddy. I want to make sure they got the news. I also want to make it clear they are welcome any time. They need to be assured that we will take good care of Melanie. I'm sure she will want to stay in her own house."

"By all means, call the Coxes." Kitty tells him, "I'm going out to the garden."

Tom says, "Wait a few minutes and I'll go with you."

Smiling at Tom she says, "I'll wait." But she thought, *Waiting for someone to go with me is all I do. Maybe with the war, Melanie and Tom will let me do more than be a conversation piece!*

CHAPTER 70

The bunk house was so quiet, you could hear a pin drop. Rowdy sat staring at his hands and finally says, "I'm going out to Mary's. This may be the last time I'll see her for a long time, because, I'm going to join the army in the morning."

"I'd join also," John says, "but I think I'm too old. I do think I'll go over to the Coxes, to see if they are okay. The rest of you guys will have to decide what you want to do. Of course, you know, not everyone will be accepted by the service. Some will have medical problems. Some will be too old or too young. I know for a fact if you are color blind, you can't join the navy. The army doesn't want you if you have flat feet. I'm very sure all the services will overlook some things. I'll see you guys later."

***

Jeff called the bunk house, only to find he had missed Rowdy. He thought, *Okay, I missed Rowdy, so I'll call Mary. I want them to go to Louisville with me. They can stand up with Susan and me. I want to get married today, because, I'm joining the navy tomorrow.*

***

All the girls were gathered in the recreation room at the YWCA. Susan was shocked and decided to return to her room. Just as she opens the door, she hears the phone ringing. Picking up the receiver, she says, "Hello."

"Susan, honey, have you heard the news?"

"Oh it's terrible. Susan answers, "Everyone here is too stunned to talk or they are being irrational. It's so confusing. Please, Jeff, I need you to hold me. Please, come."

"I'm on my way after I call Rowdy and Mary. Let's get married today. I'm joining the navy first thing in the morning. I'll see you in a little while."

"I love you. Please hurry."

"I will. Bye for now, love."

"Bye."

***

Jeff thought, *I'll drive over to Mary's instead of calling. I know Rowdy will try to talk me out of getting married. But I feel if anything happens to me, at least Susan and I will have the one night together as husband and wife, maybe more if they don't order me to camp for a few days.*

***

Susan kept pacing the lobby floor, wringing her hands, and glancing at her watch every few minutes. *I wish Jeff would hurry up,* she thought. *I'm not sure it's a good idea to marry today without mom and dad being here. I should have called them but I just want Jeff to hold me.*

Jeff stepped into the lobby of the WYCA and before he could say a thing, Susan rushed into Jeff's arms crying, "Oh, Jeff, it's horrible. I don't want you to join the navy. I don't want our life disrupted by this war. Please tell me our lives won't be touched by this war."

"I can't do that, honey. I know this will be hard for both of us, but I can't do any less. Our country needs me. Let's go and call your parents. I'm sure they'll tell you to marry me."

Rowdy interjected, "We could make this a double wedding with Mary and me as your witness and you and Jeff as our witness. What do you say?"

"I know" Mary says, "this isn't the wedding you planned or the honeymoon you imaged, but the main thing is we'll marry the love of our lives. Think how romantic our weddings will sound to our children."

Susan says, "Let's call mom and dad, and if they say to marry you, I will. Please understand, Jeff, having my parents' approval is very important to me."

Jeff grabs Susan, kisses her and says, "What are we waiting for? Let's call your parents."

CHAPTER 71

Sam Brown wasted no time in calling Tom Smith. As soon as Tom answered the phone, Sam says, "Hi, Tom, Sam Brown here."

"What's up, Sam?"

"Our Susan is getting married today, as soon as Janet and I get there. We know Kitty can't travel, but maybe Melanie would like to go, if Kitty could do without her for 24 hours."

"Yes, Sam we could do without her. I really don't think she'll go, but I'll ask and either she or I will call you back. Give Susan my best regards, and we'll send a wedding present later."

"Okay, Tom, Bye."

***

The Brown's are busy packing for the trip, when the phone rings.

Mrs. Brown calls out, "I'll get it. Hello."

"Mrs. Brown, this is Melanie. Thanks for asking me to go with you and Mr. Brown to Susan's wedding. James hasn't called me yet, and even if he had, I still wouldn't go, in case he could come home or I could go to him. Tell mom and dad, if you see them, I love them both and when they get a chance, come see me. Thanks again. I wish Susan as much happiness as James and I have. I'll send a present later."

CHAPTER 72

This isn't the wedding I always dreamed of, thought Susan. *Anyway, I'll be married to the love of my life. Mom and dad will be there. I wish Melanie had come, but I do understand that she needs to be where she can hear from James. I'm not sure how brave I will be when Jeff leaves. Tradition says the bridegroom isn't to see the bride before the wedding. I guess Jeff will see me, because we are going across the river to Jeffersonville, Indiana. There's a marriage parlor, and it stays open 24 hours. The parlor furnishes the marriage license, preacher (or is he a Justice of the Peace?), organist, the photographer, and the witness, if you don't have anyone to stand up with you. Well, it's time to go downstairs to meet Jeff, Mary, and Rowdy. I wonder if Mary and Rowdy will get married tonight. Dad and mom want to meet us at the Brown Hotel.*

Jeff watches Susan descend the stairs, he thinks, *I certainly am lucky. Look at her. She looks like a big doll. My red rose corsage is going to look great on her blue suit.*

Walking over to the bottom step and taking hold of Susan's hand, Jeff says, "Hello, the future Mrs. Jeff Spencer."

Slipping into his arms and lifting her face for his kiss, Susan says softly, "Hi, honey."

After a short kiss, Jeff tells her, "Mary and Rowdy will meet us in the lobby of the Brown Hotel. Mary's father and her aunt Grace are meeting us also."

"It sounds like we'll have a small party for our wedding, won't we."

Jeff answers, "Yes, darling, I hope when we celebrate our 25th anniversary, we can renew our vows with the party you wanted for our wedding."

Susan, with a toss of her head says, "I'll count the days until the party takes place."

Laughing, Jeff says, "You do that, however, I didn't know you could count that high."

Susan sticks out her tongue and says, "I'm sure you'll teach me, won't you."

"Sure, honey, I'll even start marking the calendar for you."

Susan turns away and says, "I need to talk to the receptionist for a minute, then we'll go."

CHAPTER 73

Everyone was waiting in the lobby of the Brown Hotel, when Susan and Jeff walked in. Mrs. Spencer says, while hugging Jeff, "I never thought I'd watch my son elope. Isn't it customary if you elope, your parents and friends aren't invited?"

Everyone laughed and Tom Brown says, "Okay, let's get this show on the road." And taking charge assigns the people to the cars. "Mary, you and Rowdy will go with your dad and your aunt Grace. Jeff, you and Susan will go with your parents. Mr. and Mrs. Cox will go with us. Now, who knows where the marriage parlor is located?"

Mrs. Cox says, "I do."

To which Mr. Spencer, with tongue in cheek asks, "Have you used it before?"

"No, why would you think that? Mrs. Cox replies, "I got directions from the desk clerk."

"I'm sorry," Mr. Spencer apologizes, "My attempt to be funny came out wrong. Please accept my apology."

"That's okay," Mrs. Cox says, "I shouldn't be so touchy."

***

On the way back to the hotel, they stop at a small restaurant for coffee and to reminisce about the wedding.

"That was a nice wedding, wasn't it?" Mr. Brown asks,

"Yes, it was, Mrs. Brown answers, "I was expecting to see 'Marrying Sam' but the Justice of the Peace looked nothing like 'Marrying Sam.'"

"Mrs. Brown, I don't want to seem ignorant, but who is 'Marring Sam?'" Mrs. Spencer asks.

Mrs. Brown answers, "I'm sorry. I always assume everyone reads the comics, because I like the comics. 'Marrying Sam' is a fat, small, preacher in the comic strip Li'l Abner. He carries his

Bible with him and is always trying to marry Li'l Abner to Daisy Mae. They all live in Dogpatch. I think the strip is funny."

Susan says, "I'm glad the Justice of the Peace was thin and tall. Otherwise, I would have started laughing.

"The marriage parlor wasn't anything like I thought it would be. It was just a plain cottage in downtown Jeffersonville. The sign outside was so gaudy, but what a difference inside."

Mrs. Brown says, "Yes, it was. I was surprised the parlor was set up like a small church. After we were seated, Mrs. Jones put the white rug down for Susan to walk on. Didn't Mrs. Jones play the organ well?"

"The wedding was very nice, Can you imagine how surprised Mr. Dearing and his sister were, when Rowdy asked if Mr. Dearing would mind, if he and Mary got married?" Mrs. Cox says.

"Jeff is going to enlist in the navy tomorrow and Rowdy is enlisting in the army." Mrs. Spencer states. "I hope the girls can go with them."

"Susan checked about jobs on all the navy bases, Jeff might be sent to." Mrs. Brown tells them. "They told her, they always have openings, because the wives go home, when their husbands go to sea."

"That's great news." Mrs. Spencer says.

CHAPTER 74

Melanie has tried to be calm, but she has twisted her hair, paced the floor, and prayed. She is thinking, *how much longer before I hear from you, James. This is almost as bad as the day you asked me to marry you.* The phone rings and she runs to answer. "Hello."

"Honey, we are being sent to the war zone. Since they aren't telling us which front, you won't be able to join me. Also, I won't get to see you before I leave. I've mailed you a letter with my address. Please write me and no matter what happens, remember, I love you and you are my life."

"Oh, James, I'll write every day. I'm so thankful we have had the last few months together. We'll have a lot more after the war. I'll stay here and continue taking care of your mother. Just remember I love you and I'll be praying for your safe return."

"Melanie, you're always in my thoughts and prayers, I love you. May God bless and keep you safe from harm. Sorry, hon, but I've got to go."

"Bye until later. I love you." Melanie hangs the phone up and prays, *Please, God, let this war end soon, and keep James safe from harm. Please God, bring James home soon. I ask this in Jesus' name. Amen.*

Yes, Melanie thought, *life does have a way of changing your plans.*

About the Author

Teddi has lived in Southern Indiana all her life. She started writing professionally after taking a couple of Creative Writing Courses at Indiana University Southeast. She has also attended several writing conferences.

Her father was a minister and Teddi took his sermons to heart. She hopes her books are an inspiration to everyone. She tells everybody, "I hope my books brings back a lot of happy memories for anyone living during World War II; and may the books help the young people cope with their loved ones leaving for combat duty."

Also from BlackWyrm...

AFTERTHOUGHTS
by Lynn Tincher

Detective Paige Aldridge was found beaten and without any memories of the previous few months. When her nephew is found dead a year later, she begins to have terrifying flashbacks, plus visions of the murders of her own family! As her loved ones begin falling prey to a serial killer, Paige believes that she must be going mad. With her family dying around her and dark suspicions forming in her mind, Paige has to pull the pieces together before it's too late.
[Psychic Crime Thriller, ages 14+]

The Holler
by Marge Fulton

The Holler hits you hard, lets you catch your breath, and then hits you again. This collection of creepy Appalachian short stories will tingle your spine and stick with you for days, with just the right mix of horrific and normal. From her experience living there, the author brings to eerie life the strangeness that is.
[Horror Short Stories, ages 14+]

LaVergne, TN USA
04 March 2011
218689LV00002B/22/P